WESTLY

WESTLY

A SPIDER'S TALE

BRYAN BEUS

SHADOW
MOUNTAIN

To my mother and father

Visit us at ShadowMountain.com

Library of Congress Cataloging-in-Publication Data
Beus, Bryan, author, illustrator.
   Westly : a spider's tale / written and illustrated by Bryan Beus.
      pages cm
   Summary: Westly is as ready as his caterpillar friends to keep their beautiful territory free of lesser creatures as they await the day they turn into delicate butterflies, but when he finally emerges from his cocoon, he discovers he is vastly different from his friends.
   ISBN 978-1-62972-068-5 (hardbound : alk. paper)
   [1. Friendship—Fiction. 2. Prejudices—Fiction. 3. Spiders—Fiction. 4. Butterflies—Fiction. 5. Moths—Fiction. 6. Race relations—Fiction.] I. Title.
   PZ7.1.B5We 2015
   [Fic]—dc23   2015010488

Printed in the United States of America
Publishers Printing

10 9 8 7 6 5 4 3 2 1

Chapter 1

Near the base of a dead volcano at the edge of a distant island stood a small glass menagerie. Clouds passed overhead, lit at the edges by the rising sun. Shielded from the outside elements, the plants, trees, and bushes grew thick and green inside the square building. Sunlight filtered through the domed ceiling and illuminated a chandelier hanging in the center of the room. Brilliant gold and white flowers covered the chandelier and filled the space right up to the edge.

As the morning sun rose, light streamed through the high menagerie windows, illuminating both the wide-open mouths of flower cups and the abundant angel ivy covering the chandelier. Waterfalls trickled from leaf pools, and the stream they formed traveled all the way from the top of the chandelier down to its edge and then tumbled out of sight. Exotic flowers grew around the crystals, creating an unorganized but beautiful garden.

At the highest level of the chandelier, several young caterpillars splashed in puddles and slid on slippery leaves. Some played under a sprinkler attached to the menagerie's water pipes.

An energetic and chubby caterpillar with a delicate jaw stood on a ledge in front of a dozen other caterpillars who were watching in anticipation. She held two leaves as if they were wings. "This is me, in style," crooned Sara, waving the leaves on her back. She leaped from her three-inch perch and landed with a bounce on her fat belly.

Another caterpillar, with round cheeks and a double chin, pointed at the bud of an exotic flower and, with a heavy nod, proclaimed, "When I get my wings, the first thing I'm going for is nectar straight from the tap!"

"I just want to soak my wings in the sun," said a third, stretching her arms out wide. They ran together in circles around the garden, leaping on top of each other, singing songs, and swinging from their caterpillar threads—all but one.

A scrawny purple caterpillar sat near the others, but he paid his silly friends no attention as he gobbled down a leaf three times his size. His eyes and teeth were bright, but otherwise

he was so dark and withered he looked like a charred piece of
wood.

"Come *on*, Westly . . . I mean, Your Majesty," Sara said.
She twirled and landed next to him with a plop. "It's our last
chance to play as caterpillars. Tomorrow we'll all be delicate
like the rest of the butterfly grown-ups."

"*Last chance* is right," Westly said, wiping the corners of his
mouth. Speaking loud enough so all could hear, he exclaimed,
"It's our last chance to juice up before our change! Tomorrow,
once our wings have taken shape in our cocoons, they'll be
that way forever. That's why you should be eating with me,
instead of goofing off. Seriously, Sara, you should sit next to
me and have some of my angel ivy," suggested Westly, tearing
off a piece.

Sara had a soft spot for her scrawny friend. She sighed.
"Yes, Your Highness." She gave a halfhearted salute before
grabbing some ivy. She opened her mouth to take a bite.

"Dirt eater!" a classmate yelled, pointing at the empty air.

"Where?" Sara dropped her ivy and jumped to her feet.

There was nothing to see, but the other caterpillars still
formed a mock battalion. Assuming it was part of a game, Sara
played along. She gasped, putting her hands to her cheeks, and
then called out, "Intruders! Fire the sprinklers!" And with that,
she ran off with the other caterpillars.

"Hey! Hey, everyone!" Westly shouted after them. When they didn't respond, he grumbled, "They'll be sorry tomorrow when their wings are smaller than mine."

The others charged playfully into the leaves. Westly sighed, hurriedly finished the last few bites of his meal, and marched after them. They scurried through the bushes, tiptoed across a narrow bridge, and wove their way through the leaves, all while throwing things at their imaginary invaders.

Just as they passed out of view, Westly heard a soft cry of alarm. He perked upright and bounded toward the sound.

As he hurried down the path to a familiar clearing, Sara darted out from behind a leaf. She placed a hand over Westly's mouth to silence him, and then pulled him back into the leaves, where all the other caterpillars were hiding.

Westly gave Sara a scowl. "What are you—"

"Shh, Your Majesty."

"But why are we . . . oh!" Westly's eyes shifted to the clearing, where a moth was sleeping in the sunlight.

A quiet gasp came from the caterpillars.

"There really *is* a dirt eater here!" whispered Westly. He stood, threw his arms in the air, and shouted, "Everyone! Drive him out! He doesn't belong here!"

In a wing beat, the moth awoke. His body went rigid when

he heard the charging caterpillars, and he fluttered into the leaves.

"Charge!" yelled a caterpillar.

"Yeah, let's catch him. It'll be fun!" yelled Sara as she bounded after the fugitive moth.

His friends, ordinary caterpillars, inched forward as fast as their small chubby bodies would allow. Every now and then, they used the threads they produced to help themselves down high ledges.

Westly, however, was anything but ordinary. Instead of scrunching and pushing like an inchworm, he scurried in a smooth fashion, his feet stepping not two at a time, but alternating from side to side like a blindingly fast centipede—and he could leap farther than anyone else. Stranger still, Westly could sling his thread and swing from leaf to leaf like a trapeze artist. His abilities raised some eyebrows, but since he was the son of the king, the others simply accepted the oddity.

The panicked moth made several attempts to fly away, but Westly blocked him from reaching the top of the ivy, and each time the other caterpillars forced the moth closer to the outer rim of the chandelier.

Upon seeing the ledge and a chance for freedom, the moth spent a final burst of energy, outpacing all but one of his relentless pursuers.

Westly was within range of the fleeing creature. The moth passed the last tuft of leaves and jumped into the open air, his wings outstretched. Before Westly reached the edge, he skidded to a halt. He watched the moth intently as it flapped frantically into the empty air below.

In one fluid motion, Westly lashed his thread to the ground and ran back a few paces just as his classmates caught up with him. They crowded around the ledge, watching the moth fly away.

"Aww, gnatters," Sara moaned as she watched the moth drop to freedom. "Wait . . . Westly? What are you doing? Westly, stop!"

As the other caterpillars watched in shock, Westly dashed toward the edge and leaped into the air after the moth, his webbed thread streaming out from behind him "Westly! You'll fall into the well!" Sara warned.

His face grim, Westly flew after the moth like a heat-seeking missile. Suddenly he realized where he was headed and his mouth opened in shock.

Far below the chandelier was a wide, black, and seemingly bottomless well covered with moss and creeping vines. Trails of steam rose from its depths and the wood holding the stones together was rotten and splintered. The ground surrounding the well was dead and dry, empty of the green life that filled the rest of the menagerie.

Just as Westly drew level with the moth, he lost his nerve and missed his chance to grab his target. Instead, he zoomed down below the creature.

The thread trailing behind Westly caught a flower's root dangling underneath the chandelier. The sticky string twisted and Westly swung in a wide circle.

As luck would have it, the thread caught the moth and pulled him along as well. In an ever-tightening circle, Westly spun around one of the chandelier's bottom struts, wrapping up the moth as he did.

Round and round they went until Westly slammed into a clump of low-hanging roots and completely disappeared.

"Westly? Your Highness!" Sara yelled from high above. The other caterpillars peered over the edge to see if they could see their fallen prince.

With great effort, Westly untangled himself from the roots and shook dirt off his head.

"Are you okay?" Sara called.

Barely. Westly nodded. He looked down at the moss-covered well waiting to swallow him whole. He gulped and looked away. He spotted the dirt eater they'd been chasing, tangled in Westly's thread. "I caught him! I have him wrapped up!" Westly shouted and began climbing over to his prisoner.

The moth struggled wildly against the thread, beating his wings and tugging with his thin legs. The more he tried to escape, the more entangled he became.

When Westly arrived, the moth finally slumped and lay still, panting heavily.

Westly boldly exclaimed, "You know you're not welcome here. The atrium is our area. You're supposed to . . ." He paused. The moth's wings were freshly tattered and chipped, and missing flakes were stuck in the tangled threads. Westly's face flushed as he realized that in capturing the moth, he had damaged his wings.

The moth growled, "I'd be happy to get out of this smelly palace if you'd just let me out of this murderous noose."

The young prince stammered, "I-I-I d-didn't mean to hurt you. I'm really s-sorry about your wings."

Westly felt a shadow of shame fall upon him—and then realized it was more than just a feeling; it was an actual shadow passing overhead. He and the moth looked up. Above them a majestic butterfly blocked the sun, the light illuminating its translucent wings like fire. The large butterfly fluttered into view—a monarch butterfly. Westly immediately recognized the crown that adorned the butterfly's head and the velvet robe wrapped around his neck and shoulders.

"Father!" Westly exclaimed.

The moth shuddered.

"What in heaven's name?" the Monarch began, throwing his robe over his shoulder. "Is that a creature from the undergrowth . . . in *our* territory?"

The old moth harrumphed.

"And what are you doing holding him here, my boy?" demanded the Monarch.

"Well, um, it was an accident," Westly said. "I was only trying to chase him away." The Monarch turned from his son to the unwelcome moth. He puffed out his chest. "And what were you doing in my kingdom? You have no right to be here!"

The moth only struggled harder against his bonds.

"Get him out of here!" the Monarch commanded.

Westly carefully but quickly began to unwind his thread. He didn't want to cause any further damage to the moth.

The Monarch tapped his hands together impatiently.

Finally, the last of Westly's thread came loose. The moth wasted no time fluttering for the trees.

As Westly watched him go, the moth turned his head back. Their eyes met and Westly felt an electric thrill pass through his body, but he couldn't understand why.

"I'll bet my spots he was coming to drink our nectar," the Monarch huffed. He turned to Westly. "And a prince should not be mingling with riffraff."

"I was just trying to—" Westly started, cringing.

"It's not befitting a prince to be caught with such hooligans. Our subjects might start thinking you're *friendly* with them, and that sort of rumor would spread like pondside moss." There was nothing more to say, and Westly shrank further.

"Well," the Monarch said, "I'm sure you'll learn eventually."

"Yes, Father. I promise," Westly replied.

The Monarch put his arm around his only son. "I am proud of you, Westly. But come to me next time, child. The well-being of the chandelier depends upon us, upon the way we respond to threats like this. And someday it will depend entirely upon you. Understood?"

Westly nodded.

"Good. Now climb on my back and I'll get you to the palace. I'll expect you in the auditorium before the cocoon ceremony begins. Today is your big day!"

Chapter 2

The inside of the chandelier featured a large circular courtyard made from vines and other flowering plants. It was where all the butterflies gathered in preparation for the cocoon ceremony. Dinner had been served, and Westly was gorging himself. Instead of eating the richly filling rose petals or lily pollen, he had chosen the more common but nutritious greens. Frankly, he was tired of angel ivy and milkweed, but he forced himself to keep eating. He ignored his classmates, who were too excited and nervous to eat sensibly. Instead, they gulped down sweet nectar desserts. Black-and-white butterflies offered trays of white rose petals, lilac stems, and tiny purple amaranth flowers.

Sitting on leaves at the edge of the chandelier, the caterpillars nibbled bites from the dessert trays and pestered the adults with question after question about their ceremony and about how the transformation would feel.

A blue-spotted butterfly replied, "Stop worrying. This is the most important day of your lives. Enjoy the moment!"

Some butterflies uncurled their long noses to play like flutes, and others beat their wings in wild rhythms, shaking so that their thin antennae twirled around in hypnotizing patterns.

As Westly slowly finished another leaf, Sara noticed him sitting alone. As much as he had eaten, his little body was not as plump as one might expect. She inched over to her friend and said, "Prince Westly, I would be honored to dance with you."

As Westly looked up, he clutched his stomach, his cheeks turned purple, and he doubled over.

"Are you all right?" Sara asked. She bent to look at Westly's face.

"I'm quite all right, thank you very much," Westly gasped, turning his head and wincing. Before she could reply, Westly's cheeks bulged and he ran for the exit, clutching at his thin crown to keep it from slipping off his head.

He ran through a tunnel in the ivy and emerged on the outer rim of the chandelier. He quickly leaned over the edge and relieved his aching stomach.

Suddenly, he felt an odd tingling sensation at the base of his skull. It felt like he was being watched. He clamped his mouth shut and looked up.

Outside the glass windows, the silhouette of a large bird stared down at Westly. Protected by the glass menagerie all his life, Westly had never seen a bird before. It was a very strange and dreamlike vision. *Are my eyes playing tricks on me?*

His stomach gurgled and he bent over the edge again.

A soft voice from within the ivy said, "Your Highness? Westly, are you there?" Westly wiped his mouth and clutched his stomach.

"There you are," Sara said. "Are you all right? You're missing the Silken Sisters, and they almost never play in public."

Westly straightened up, stretched his arms, and smiled. "After tomorrow, I can command them to play again. You'll just have to ask me nicely." He winked.

Sara smiled and spun around on a leaf. "What were you doing out here?"

"Oh—um, I saw something and wanted to see what it was.

As a butterfly prince, it'll be my job, you know, to watch over the safety of the chandelier."

"What'd you see?"

"I—well—I don't know. It was up there." Westly pointed out to the atrium. "I'm going to investigate."

"You mean it was outside the windows?" Sara hopped to the ground, her eyes bright with excitement. "I've never seen anything out there. Can I tag along?"

"No." Westly shook his head.

"Why not?"

"Because it's probably dangerous."

"But there's glass."

"Still. I might die, you know."

Sara pursed her lips.

"I'm not joking," Westly insisted.

"All right, I believe you," Sara sighed, sitting down. "Can I wait here, Your Majesty, so you can tell me about it when you get back?"

"*If* I get back," Westly said.

"All right, *if* you get back?"

"That's a good question," Westly mused, running a hand over his thin crown. "The problem is—what if I don't *ever* come back? You'd be waiting here all night."

Sara raised an eyebrow.

Westly huffed. "Well, all right then. You can come along—"

She smiled widely.

"—and in the event of my untimely death, it'll be your job to take my crown back to my father and tell him what happened. That way they can all write songs about how I died as a hero, defending our kingdom from outside invaders."

"Okay!" she exclaimed, bouncing to her feet.

"Right. Okay, well, this way, then," Westly said, pointing to the ceiling, and the two marched off through the brush.

A quarter of an hour later, they reached the stem of the chandelier and climbed up a few inches. With no flowers or leaves to block their view, they could see the night sky.

"Keep your eyes there," said Westly, pointing at the spot on the glass where he had seen the shadow of the bird.

The two caterpillars settled down to wait. A minute passed. There was nothing but stars. "I'll bet it's out there and we just can't see it," Westly whispered, still searching.

Another few minutes passed, and then Sara quietly sighed.

"I really did see it," Westly said.

"I believe you," Sara replied.

"It was big—bigger than the highest tier of the chandelier. And it had red glowing eyes and yellow claws."

Sara squinted at him.

"Don't you believe me?"

"I already said I did, didn't I?" she said, gently swinging her lower feet.

"Well, it's gone now," Westly said. "So there's no point in staying here any longer. Let's go back to the party."

"Yes, Your Majesty," Sara murmured. She let go of the stem and fell to the ground with a plop.

Chapter 3

The cocoon ceremony was the most important time of the year. For the caterpillars, there was nothing greater than the day they revealed their true colors. In fact, the color of their wings determined much of the rest of their lives. A butterfly's wings had to complement specific flowers in the chandelier, which determined the level the butterfly would live in. Those born to the highest rank—usually those with ultramarine blue wings—were selected for the king's council, blue being the natural complementary color to the monarch's orange.

Unlike the other caterpillars, who were anxious about the change, Westly was more anxious about what would come after that. It was no secret to him what he would look like: all monarchs' wings were a similar mix of orange and black with white spots. What concerned him most was the responsibility he would have as a butterfly prince.

His father reminded Westly often that as the prince, he would be responsible for the future of the chandelier and those who lived in it. *But what if I make a mistake? What if I lose the respect of the others? What if our chandelier home is overrun with weeds? It would all be my fault.*

Westly swallowed his fear and reminded himself that once he had traded his small caterpillar body for his butterfly wings, the mere presence of those great and noble monarch wings would command others' respect. He would make his father and his fellow butterflies proud.

When the dancing and the party ended, all the caterpillars gathered in the center of the courtyard. Leaves had been deliberately hung in rows, one for each of the graduating caterpillars. One by one, the members of Westly's class chose the place where they would change. Westly made his way to a particularly large leaf hung over a bed of milkweed, the royal mark of the monarchs.

"Ladies and gentle creatures, girls and boys," Westly's father's voice boomed across the courtyard. The Monarch fluttered into the center of the graduating class. "How grateful I am to have you here this evening. As you know, we've waited for this day since you were born. Above you now are the ceremonial leaves upon which you will change from caterpillars to butterflies. You have earned your right to transform, and it is into your hands that we now entrust our honor, nobility, and tradition."

There were grins all around from butterfly and caterpillar alike.

"Now the time has come for you to make your way through the cocoon's womb. I can see that you all are prepared in your hearts, but are confused as to how you will achieve this change. And though you have asked time and time again, we have always refused to tell you the method by which you will create this delicate shell."

A knowing smile rippled through the adults as they recalled their own experience.

"It is not for our generation to guide you from here," the Monarch continued. "From this day on, you must create your own path. We will not always be here to guide you. However, you will not be entirely without guidance. Among you is a leader, one whose task it is to break the mold of this caterpillar skin of yours and bring you into the new world of flight and beauty."

The Monarch turned to his son.

All eyes shifted to Westly.

The prince, who was quite accustomed to his father giving speeches, was sitting with his legs sprawled and his chin in his hands. With the entire kingdom suddenly staring at him, Westly felt as though he were trapped in a lamp. To make sure he understood his father correctly, Westly pointed at his chest and glanced as though to ask, *Me?*

The Monarch gave Westly a warm smile.

His heart pounding, Westly nodded, stood up, and took a deep breath. "Okay. Yes. I will now instruct you, um, in how to create your cocoon."

He held his hands out toward his classmates and straightened his spine.

All the caterpillars followed suit.

Nervous, Westly took another deep breath.

They all copied him.

This made Westly hold his breath.

His friends did the same.

Not knowing what he was supposed to do, Westly shook out his hands and closed his eyes. He remembered learning that each caterpillar had a cocoon already formed within his own body. But how to get his body to shed its skin and bring the cocoon out? Westly didn't know. There had to be some kind of trigger.

He opened his eyes again.

Everyone was still staring at him.

Westly bit his tongue. There was no reason why this should be more difficult for him than it was for anyone else, Monarch's son or not. But he needed to do something—anything—while he figured it out.

"All right. So, you take your hands," he said, moving them to his head. "And place them on your antennae"—he grabbed hold of his own—"and . . . you pull really hard . . ."

He closed his eyes and pulled his sensitive antennae wide, until the skin on his head stretched tight.

Opening one eye, he saw all his classmates around him gritting their teeth and yanking hard. Jane, a female caterpillar in his class, whispered "Ow!" as she popped off an antenna. Luckily for her she'd regrow it in her cocoon.

"Okay. G-g-good," Westly stammered. "So, now that we've done that, we, uh . . . we take our thread and attach one end to our seats. Yes, and we wrap it around our feet . . . and then we keep spinning around and around. Yes! We keep doing that until we've made a cocoon like this."

Westly continued spinning in circles, wrapping his thread

higher and higher around his body, sensing all the while that the other caterpillars, doubting his knowledge, had stopped copying him and were watching to see what would happen.

"And once we're done with that, we're going to reach up, attach the thread to our leaves, swing upside down, and hang—" With as much confidence as he could muster, Westly did just that. Instead of hanging securely, however, his thread immediately began to unravel, spinning Westly around so quickly the atrium clearing turned into a blur of lights. In a moment his thread ran out and he fell off the leaf, crashing into a patch of milkweed leaves.

"Westly?" a classmate called. "Aren't our cocoons supposed to be a hard shell? I didn't think—"

"That's how you do it," Westly said, holding up a hand. "I just forgot something—"

"Hey, something's happening to my tail!" Sara exclaimed.

Everyone turned to her.

Indeed, her tail was producing a sticky substance.

"I feel . . . *funny*," she said, almost as if in a trance. Softly, she pressed her tail to the underside of her leaf, where it stuck like glue. She swung upside down to hang.

Closing her eyes, she sighed deeply, and then her body bulged like a balloon. The caterpillars gasped.

She opened her eyes briefly, and said with a smile, "All you have to do is relax . . . and just let it happen."

In another moment, her body swelled up again. This time she winced until the pressure released. She panted a few times, and then her head and body inflated until her grin was almost as large as her head usually was. She kept growing and enlarging and expanding until, with a gentle *pop*, the skin split down the middle of her face. Her body returned to its normal size, but her skin began to slip away, falling to the floor and revealing a sparkling green cocoon hanging from the leaf. The other caterpillars watched with amazement, some turning to each other with raised eyebrows and pleasantly grossed-out smirks.

Before long another caterpillar relaxed himself and began the change, and then another, and by the time Westly finished climbing back to his leaf and arranging himself to hang upside down, he was one of the only caterpillars not yet changing.

Taking great care not to make eye contact with his father, he briefly closed his eyes. He tried clearing his mind, but the humiliation of his first failure buzzed in his head. After a few minutes, Westly managed to finally calm himself down. Seeing that everyone else had begun their change, and everything was okay, Westly took a deep breath and exhaled slowly. Finally, the strange sticky substance emerged from his tail too.

He took one last glance at all the other bright green

cocoons and then closed his eyes as he had seen the others do. A massive pressure—like a balloon expanding inside his neck—caused him to gasp. It lasted only a second before it was gone, only to be repeated again, even stronger, and then a third time. On the fourth time, there was such a powerful force within his head that for a moment he thought he might explode. A deafening *pop* filled his head, and then it was over.

The last thing he remembered was catching a brief glimpse of his own cocoon, the most brilliant white he had ever seen. Then he fainted.

Chapter 4

L adies and gentle creatures, let the grand metamorphosis ceremony begin!"

Westly woke with a start. He tried to stretch but gasped in pain. His whole body felt like a peach pit stuck inside its fruit. His spine burned like a twig pulled apart and then rolled back together. Every muscle cramped as he tested his legs, but it was too much to bear, so he stayed still.

Music exploded all around Westly. Even though the cocoon muffled the sound, the music was so loud it hurt his ears. He heard wings flapping in rhythm, voices singing, and noses blasting like trumpets. Westly tried once more to move his arms, and this time he succeeded in pulling his hand up to his eyes. He picked a small hole in his cocoon's shell so he could watch the display.

The king's counselors fluttered their royal blue wings and sipped at nectar in flower cups. The cocoons of his classmates glimmered in the morning light. The dancing rainbow lights of the chandelier were everywhere. He had never seen so many butterflies gathered together all at once, and everyone was so happy, too. After what seemed like an hour, Westly's father's voice rose over the sounds of the party.

"Good creatures," the Monarch began, standing up from his golden throne, "I see signs of movement in the cocoons. Several cracks are even appearing! It is time for our young ones to emerge."

All the butterflies in the air slowly found their seats where they sipped their leftover cups of nectar.

"I remind you to wait to join your children until *after* their wings harden."

From somewhere to Westly's left he heard a painful crack, presumably from a cocoon. From the audience came an admiring *Oooh*.

Westly twisted his body back and forth, and his cocoon slowly rocked and turned until he saw the cocoon next to him wiggling somewhat violently. A large crack appeared on the bottom, spreading slowly up the side of the crisp outer shell. Flakes fell away, the opening at the bottom widened, and then the familiar antennae and head of Westly's friend Sara popped out of her shell. She panted heavily for a moment until, finally, she managed to pull all of her slender new body free of the shattered cocoon. Her crumpled pink wings drooped toward the ground for a moment before she stretched them out to their full size.

"Splendid! As beautiful as can be," cried the Monarch.

By now more than half a dozen of the other cocoons were squirming and rocking. The Monarch could barely keep track of them. The new butterflies emerged, slowly and painfully, to reveal a rainbow of colors—white speckled wings; purple polka-dots; brown and dusty gray spots; pine-yellow with black freckles at the tips; ultramarine and orange spots on the wings that looked like eyes staring out at the audience.

Cracking continued as the young butterflies broke their shells; the audience applauded each time one emerged. At first, Westly wanted to wait to be last so he could make the most dramatic appearance. But as he watched all his peers smiling and chattering about their new wings, Westly's patience ran out and he began to press against the walls of his cocoon.

"Here comes another," shouted the Monarch. Westly thought he detected an extra hint of pride in his father's voice.

He wiggled in his shell, pushing against the sides as hard as he could, starting where he had already poked a hole. *Crack!* The angel-white cocoon began to open.

The audience oohed, and their encouragement increased Westly's confidence. He pressed his hands and feet harder against the rip in the cocoon.

Another crack, and then another, and soon the top of his head broke through. He caught a glimpse of his father, proudly waving his arms to get everyone to look.

With another push, the top four of Westly's legs broke through. The edges of the cocoon scratched lightly at his tender legs.

The Monarch was positively brimming with pride, and he cheered, "That's my boy! Look at him go! Prince . . . Westly!"

With all eyes on him, Westly gave another push, and then something unusual happened: instead of one more pair of butterfly legs popping out, there were four.

The audience cheered for a brief moment, and then their faces changed to confusion as they counted to themselves.

Eight legs?

Westly was so busy trying to get out of his shell that he hadn't noticed his extra set of legs. The air filling his lungs was as delicious to him as splashing in a pool of nectar. More than anything he wanted to be free of his shell.

His friends encircled him with their beautiful wings, and the audience stared with wide-eyed anticipation. He felt as though the morning light was shining only for him. There was just one more push to go. *One, two, three!* His cocoon tore away in all directions and Westly sprang from his prison, landing in front of everyone—a black, hairy, eight-legged spider.

A collective gasp rushed through the audience. Wings stopped flapping, and jaws dropped.

The Monarch stared, a confused look on his face. Westly gasped and panted, putting his hands on his knees. The audience was silent, frozen in fear.

Wheezing heavily, Westly finally raised his head and turned to look at the crowd. They didn't cheer. Instead, they stared back with eyes full of wonder.

I must look extraordinary, Westly thought. *My wings have made them speechless. I never expected to garner this much attention. Wow, this royalty thing is going to take some time getting used to.* Gleefully, Westly smiled from ear to ear, revealing sharp, pointy teeth.

Someone from the audience shrieked, "Infestation!"

"Huh?" Westly said, turning toward his father.

The Monarch stared at Westly as though he had never seen him before. He stumbled backwards and, while pointing to his son, hissed, *"Monster!"*

Mayhem erupted throughout the clearing as the butterflies attempted to escape. Some fainted, barely waking in time to avoid falling into the dark well. Others crashed madly into the vines, entangling their curly noses and legs. The clearing was a flurry of colored wings.

Confused, Westly looked around at the chaos. He turned to Sara. "Do you know what—"

But Sara also cringed and screamed, "Eww, get away!"

Finally, Westly glanced down and as he did, his eyebrows rose to the top of his head. His hands were not the delicate, elegant hands of a butterfly. His belly was not the soft fuzzy belly of a monarch. His feet were not tapered and clean, but pointy and sharp. His tail was not sleek and long, but bulbous and round. Worst of all, when he looked at his back, he saw he was entirely without wings.

With a scream, Westly realized that his change had gone horribly, terribly, wickedly wrong. He ran from his broken cocoon as if he could escape the horrid creature that had possessed him, rushing into the mass of fleeing butterflies, and fell into a courtyard pond, landing with a splash.

Shaking, terrified, Westly looked up and saw his father staring down at him with confusion, horror, and anger in his eyes.

Chapter 5

Some kind of . . . *leech*," murmured the Monarch, who had never seen such an insect before. Indeed, few butterflies had ever roamed outside the kingdom, and certainly none had encountered an eight-legged creature like this.

"Foul creature! Whence comest thou—" began the Monarch, slipping into the old tongue.

"I don't understand, Dad," Westly cried, his knees trembling.

"That you and your filth should come—" the Monarch paused. "Did you say *Dad?*"

"Please," Westly implored. "What's going on? Why is everyone so angry?"

"Westly?" the Monarch whispered.

His son shuddered and nodded.

The Monarch stumbled back with renewed horror.

"Please, Dad. Please," Westly cried, tears dripping from his nose as he crawled toward his father.

"I-I-Is that really you?" the king stuttered.

Westly buried his face in his father's robes. The Monarch looked back and saw his counselors observing them both with equal parts confusion and fear. With an uncertain glance, he turned back to his son.

"Am I dreaming, Dad? What's wrong?"

"H-how did you get like this?" the Monarch asked with deep concern.

"I don't know," Westly whimpered, looking at his back again. "Why don't I have any wings?"

"But . . . I-I . . ." The Monarch broke off, at a loss for words.

Seeing his father's uncertainty, Westly clutched his father's robes even tighter. The Monarch brushed his hand over Westly's head, and then drew it away quickly.

When Westly looked up, the Monarch was staring out at a crowd of butterflies that had stopped fleeing and returned, each trying to see what was happening.

Instinctively, Westly crawled behind his father.

"Don't worry, son," the Monarch finally said, shaking his head. "I'll . . . I'll think of something."

Westly's father instructed a few royal counselors to stand with their wings held open, creating a wall to block the crowd's view. Then he retreated several steps and began a whispered conversation with the remaining counselors.

Though Westly couldn't hear what was being said, he could read their lips to understand enough.

"How do we explain it?"

"What if they don't believe us?"

"But, certainly, butterfly or not, he can never be the Monarch. He's one of those . . . those other creatures."

With each exchange, the Monarch appeared to be increasingly unhappy. He seemed to be arguing for Westly, but he was clearly losing whatever argument he was making.

Westly turned away. He didn't want to think about it anymore. He needed to make sense of what was happening, but fears were flying too rapidly through his head. Memories filled his imagination: his healthy, chubby friends looking with concern at his withered little body; his strange ability to jump higher than everyone else and swing with his thread; his disastrous attempt to show his classmates how to change.

As each memory flashed before Westly's eyes, the anxiety in his heart grew. He wanted time to think things through, to wait until his father figured out what had happened, and to learn how he and his advisors were going to fix it.

But Westly knew there was nothing they could do. Glancing upward, he saw that his cocoon was entirely empty—there was no sign of his missing wings, antennae, or anything else. It was an empty shell. Westly had changed into something completely different than a butterfly.

He would be forever a disappointment—to his father, to his friends, to the whole kingdom. Without wings he could never, ever rule the kingdom of the butterflies. In fact, Westly didn't belong with them at all anymore. In one split second, whatever glimmer of loneliness he had felt at the thought of being a prince increased a hundredfold. He needed to make a decision, do something that would put himself back in control of his life. And he needed to do it immediately.

As his father and counselors were determining his fate, Westly carefully and quietly crawled behind his father's counselors' wings and along the southern side of the chandelier, staying well out of view. When he reached the edge, he slipped onto the trail that led through the ivy, ran without pause to the outer rim of the chandelier, snapped a thread to the edge, and leaped into the open air.

He sailed farther and farther until he landed with a crunch in the trees on the opposite side. Getting to his feet, Westly glanced backward. No one had noticed his escape.

It was the first time he had ever considered leaving the kingdom of the butterflies. Since he had been a child, the sparkling chandelier had been the place he called home, the place where he thought he belonged. But his friends and family glaring at him in shock and disgust was more than he could bear.

The forest before him was entirely empty. While the unknown would have frightened him on any other day, he was so confused and unhappy that he felt that the forest beyond could protect him from the disgust of his friends and family.

Without another thought, Westly left the light of the crystal chandelier and sprinted into the darkness.

Chapter 6

Westly crawled through the murky forest and swung from limb to limb. The shock of what had happened turned his mind blank for hours. In one moment he had lost the respect of the kingdom, the comfort of his family, and the joy of being a butterfly. He didn't question his decision to run away. How could he live with butterflies when he was a monster?

Westly stopped to rest on a gnarled branch. He had wandered through the woods for so long he had no idea what direction he was traveling. The initial shock of his unexpected transformation now gave way to fear. *Where am I? Why did I travel so far?* he scolded himself. He tried to retrace his steps, but he couldn't find the right direction.

Westly's heart raced. His lungs squeezed. He bolted madly into the dark—which is not a smart thing to do when you don't know where you're going. *Whoosh!* He ran straight off the end of the branch and into thin air. Flipping end over end as he fell, he passed through the mist and plunged down past the tall tree trunks of the menagerie forest. Eyes wide, mouth gaping, Westly fell into the deep undergrowth, landing with a *thump* on a mushy mushroom.

Splat! Squish! Smash! Westly ripped through the top of the mushroom like a wrecking ball. Pieces of mushroom scattered everywhere. Westly ended up with a large piece around his neck like a collar. He tugged and pushed until the squishy mass slipped off.

Westly took a deep breath and sighed. He rubbed his eyes and squinted to see his surroundings. There was very little light coming from the thick canopy above.

His whole body ached and there were strange sounds in the distance. "What was I thinking?" Westly moaned.

He heard something behind him and spun around. It was too misty to see more than a few feet away, but he felt sure he'd caught a glimpse of a fleeting shadow somewhere in the distance. He knew little of the dirt eaters, but the stories told among the butterflies suggested they were wild and brutal creatures.

Did something just sniff? Westly didn't wait to find out.

Scrambling through the mushrooms, he pushed and pulled his way forward until his feet finally hit wet topsoil. It was the first time in his life that he had stood on the earth itself and it felt funny. He quickly pushed the odd sensation out of his mind and ran forward.

That was a bad idea because though the earth was solid, the patch of soggy mulch he ran onto was not. Westly slipped and fell face first with a *plop*.

His back covered with bits of mushroom, his face smeared with mud, he pushed himself up and stumbled toward the safety of the undergrowth. A solid blanket of leaves gave Westly the footing he needed as he dashed forward to find somewhere he could hide.

Thud! Westly ran smack into a plant. He was stuck to a tentacle-like leaf covered with a sticky goo. Thin hairs from the plant closed around Westly's shoulders, arms, and legs. He grunted as he struggled to free himself. After a full minute of wriggling, pushing, and kicking, he slumped, exhausted. But only for a moment. He suddenly remembered learning in school about the plants in the menagerie—and a warning about carnivorous plants on the menagerie floor.

Oh no! Westly thought. *A sundew plant—I'm trapped in a lethal sundew plant!* He knew he had fewer than fifteen minutes before the slimy goo on the plant's tentacles would begin to dissolve him. His fingers and eyes were already stinging.

"Help me! Somebody! Anybody! Help!" Westly shouted.

Westly began to feel groggy. The plant was trying to put him to sleep. He fought the feeling and cried out again. "Help!"

For a split second, Westly caught a glimpse of something tiny that zipped by him and then changed directions in a flash. Whatever it was buzzed right up to his ear. Frantic, he tried to swat it away, but it was persistent. The buzzing came from one side, then the other, then above, before it finally disappeared behind him. Westly wanted to yell again but his body felt heavy and tired.

With a last bit of energy, Westly tried to push his way out of the sticky prison, but it was no use.

Something purred near Westly. It seemed as though it might be coming from the plant, but he couldn't be sure. He heard clicking, then a *poof* of smelly powder drifted overhead. Suddenly, the plant released its grasp and flicked Westly away. He shot through the air about a foot before landing on a carpet of leaves.

Westly wiped the slime off his face and ran for the nearest cover of bushes. Here's my chance to get out of here, he thought as he scrambled away.

"No, no, no! Mustn't leave. Stay, stay, stay!" a high-pitched voice squeaked.

Westly looked over his shoulder to see who was talking to

him, but he couldn't see anyone. It wasn't the sundew plant, was it?

Westly backed away slowly. Ten paces, twenty paces, thirty paces. Just as he turned around, he stepped out of the thicket of leaves and into a stream. *Splash!*

He was drowning! The water was ten times as deep as the largest pool in the chandelier. The stream moved so swiftly he couldn't catch his breath.

Twisting and tumbling, his arms and legs flailing, Westly struggled in the swirling water. Bubbles surrounded him. For a couple of seconds, his head bobbed above water, and he gasped for air. He saw the shadow of a creature with four wings and large bulbous eyes. A dragonfly? Westly had only heard of such creatures. Then a second dirt eater with large jaws—a water beetle—lunged under Westly and pushed him up from the deep. Westly couldn't remember if he'd learned in school whether beetles were dangerous or not. His heart beat faster.

The dragonfly zipped across the watery surface and snatched Westly up by his shoulders. They rocketed downstream, skimming low and swaying from side to side.

They dodged and spun through the tangle of river vines so fast that Westly promptly emptied the contents of his stomach again—straight into the water.

Westly had no idea of what had happened the last few

minutes, only that a dragonfly had captured him and was taking him somewhere. He didn't know, or care. As his eyes cleared and his mind settled, he caught a glimpse of dry land to his right. Without thinking, Westly leaned over and bit down hard on the dragonfly's claw.

The creature cried out in pain, and with a twist and a wriggle, Westly broke free. He tried to gauge where he would land but the mist was too thick and the light from the faraway canopy too dim.

Out of the frying pan and into the fire. Westly remembered his father saying that from time to time when things went from bad to worse. He was about to experience firsthand what it truly meant.

Although he had escaped from one dangerous plant, Westly fell into the gaping jaws of a much more lethal one. Upon impact, the Venus flytrap instantly closed around Westly's body with a *snap*.

Chapter 7

The flytrap's jaws were not quite as painful as the sundew's, but being trapped inside it was much scarier. For one thing, Westly couldn't see anything but the bar-like teeth holding him inside. And for another, the plant was squeezing the wind out of his lungs.

"Help," Westly gasped. "Please, help me . . ."

For a minute there was silence, and Westly thought he was doomed for sure. Then he heard a sniffing sound. Having seen the dragonfly's fangs and sharp claws up close, Westly suspected that it must be hunting him. He held his breath.

The sniffing came right up to the plant, and then the fanged creature peered through the plant's green teeth.

Its eyes were bright blue with a light green line around the top, giving a permanent sternness to its face. However, when Westly looked deeper he thought he saw genuine concern.

"Oh no," the dragonfly sighed. "There goes a full day."

"Don't touch me," Westly wheezed. "I'm warning you."

The dragonfly raised one of its bright green eyebrows and growled, "Stay still. This will take some help."

"I don't want any help—" Westly began, but the dragonfly had already vanished into the fog.

The plant seemed to clamp its mouth tighter over Westly. Spots appeared before his eyes.

Moments later, a rapidly buzzing creature zipped past the mouth of the plant and landed on its teeth to look at Westly. "Don't get eaten. Make Zug Zug sad," it squeaked, and gave Westly a sad look before it, too, disappeared.

Seeing that he had no other choice but to wait for help, Westly gritted his teeth, yet the longer he waited, the more nervous he became. Soon any sound in the forest, whether a drop of water or a leaf falling, scared him. It was all he could do to not cry out for help again.

An hour passed, maybe two. Westly lost track of the time. The sticky interior of the plant was beginning to burn his skin. He tried to be obedient and stay still, but the goo coming out of the plant felt like hot nectar salsa—the really, really, really hot kind!

Westly desperately tried to tear his way out of the plant, but his attempts were useless. Each time he moved, the plant closed tighter around him, filling every empty space, crushing him until his body was a tangled mess of legs and hands.

His lungs finally gave way as he softly cried one last time, "Help."

In the silence, Westly realized he was truly alone. He thought, *Those dirt eaters aren't coming back. They've decided a butterfly isn't worth rescuing.* Westly paused. He realized they didn't know he was a butterfly. They saw him as the monster he was. The thought made him cringe. His change had left him without his wings. And now he had an extra mutant pair of legs.

Westly's breathing was shallow. He pondered on his final thoughts. *Do I even have a purpose anymore? What good am I like this? Maybe this is exactly where I belong.*

The light grew dim, his eyes blurred, and he passed out.

Westly gasped as he tumbled out of his living coffin and landed in a bare patch of dirt. Coughing and covered in goo, he looked around at a dozen odd-looking insects standing around him, their mouths open in curious wonder. Behind him the Venus flytrap had been broken open.

In the front of the group was the stern dragonfly who had lifted Westly from the stream. On his shoulder was the tiny fly with beaming eyes.

The dragonfly looked Westly carefully over while the other insects whispered among themselves.

"Did you see it?"

"It's sitting right there, of course we did."

"But did you see it with its eyes open?"

"Shh! Quiet. It's waking up."

Westly coughed violently, pressed himself up on his hands, and spat hot pink goo out of his mouth. His tongue and lips were numb.

"What is it?" one of the creatures asked.

"Don't know. Maybe it'll tell us," another said.

"Zug Zug knows," the fly said. "It's a mushroom!"

The others groaned.

The tall dragonfly finally stepped forward. "I'm the leader of the gardeners. Saving you has cost us a whole day. Who are you, and where did you come from?"

The creatures surrounding Westly were all entirely unfamiliar to him and intimidating, and he could only stammer, "W-what?"

"You can't be one of ours. We know better than to go running into a clamper," said the dragonfly.

"What's a clamper?"

The dragonfly sighed and pointed to the mangled Venus flytrap.

"Oh, is that what it's called? I didn't know," Westly replied.

"Look, I'm lost, and when you dirt eaters started chasing me—"

"What'd you call us?" an insect at the back of the crowd demanded. It was long, slender, and had hundreds of feet.

"Oh. Uh, dirt eaters? Isn't that what you call yourselves?"

"We're *bugs!*" the insect shouted.

"Or you could call us gardeners," the dragonfly added.

Westly thought he heard someone whisper, "Knows the fuzzheads."

"Listen," the dragonfly continued, "we don't know who you are, or *what* you are. But you're doing about as well as a larva out here on your own. So if you're going to stay with us—"

"Stay with you?" interrupted Westly, surprised. He had no intention of staying with dirt eaters. But they were willing to help him, so perhaps he could consider them his neighbors for the time being. "I mean, I'm a butter—" He broke off mid-sentence and cleared his throat.

Who am I? Westly thought. *WHAT am I?*

He was a freak who didn't belong on the chandelier with the butterflies. And he certainly didn't feel at home in the dirt. As Westly looked around at the insects' confused faces, it reminded him of the horror on his father's face at the change ceremony. Westly cringed. The feeling of being a disappointment to his father, his kingdom, and himself was overwhelming. He shut his eyes tightly, took a deep breath, and exhaled slowly.

"Can you at least tell us your name?" asked the dragonfly.

"My name is Westly," he replied. "But I just, you know, hatched from . . . my shell yesterday." He knew he had to come up with a reasonable story—something besides the fact that he used to be a butterfly prince. "Er . . . well, you see, I got lost. So I decided to take a nap."

"Take a nap?" the many-footed creature scoffed, pointing at what remained of the Venus flytrap. "What, in there?"

"He's tricking us," another bug shouted. "I'll bet he's some kind of demon. A demon from the *well.*"

The other creatures gasped.

"A demon?" Westly asked.

The dragonfly squinted at him, then waved for everyone to follow him into the forest. "Just leave him here if that's what he wants. You might have said thanks for the rescue."

The creatures gave shouts of support and thumbed their noses at Westly as they began marching back into the forest.

From the back of the group a voice grumbled, "Out of the way, out of the way, I say!" A bug with brown wings and two feathery antennae made his way toward Westly.

Westly immediately recognized him as the same moth he had captured in his thread the day before. The moth came to the front of the group and shook his head. "Slow down, everyone. Don't be so quick to judge. Westly, is it? Been through a lot, this one, right?"

Westly breathed a sigh of relief. The moth hadn't recognized him. *It's no wonder,* he thought. *Westly the caterpillar is gone. And who knows what happened to Westly the butterfly.*

The moth patted Westly on the arm gently. "If he keeps it up, he won't last long out here by himself."

"That's *his* problem," the dragonfly said matter-of-factly.

The moth ignored the dragonfly. "I can't say how I know it, but there's something about him that says he deserves a chance."

Westly watched curiously as the moth bent over him and touched his face with his fuzzy antennae.

"Something familiar . . ." the moth muttered.

The moth's eyes weren't dark and deep like the other insects' eyes. Instead, they were a milky white.

"In case you're wondering, the answer is yes, I'm blind,"

the moth said, his antennae roving over Westly's face. "But I see perfectly fine with these."

He turned around. "This little fellow here might appear different to you. But he's a child of the menagerie, and, therefore, one of us."

The dragonfly folded one set of arms and rubbed his chin with a free hand. He gave the moth a brief nod. "All right. Westly, you can come with us. But you've cost us enough time already. It took a whole day's march to get everyone here so we could tear open the clamper. We move out now!"

"Excuse me," Westly interrupted, taking a step back. "I appreciate your saving me, and for agreeing not to leave me in the forest, but I'd really prefer to be alone, for now at least."

The dragonfly looked at the moth and frowned. The other insects widened their eyes in disbelief.

The moth gave a slight grin, chuckled, and shook his head as if to say, *Poor child, doesn't know what's good for him.*

Westly grimaced, not quite sure what to make of all the awkwardness. Though getting away from this group was what he wanted, their reaction scared him. "I'll just go live in the treetops, where it's safe," he said.

"Safe? Up there?" asked the moth, pointing upwards. "Is that what you think?"

"Well, if it's not safe up there, then perhaps you can tell me where I could find a good place to sleep."

The dragonfly looked at his own swarm of insects, then back at Westly, and gave him a stare more penetrating than even the Monarch could manage. "Do as you wish. And sleep where you like. It's all the same around here."

And with that he walked away, the others following close behind.

"No-no-no!" Zug Zug piped. The little fly buzzed to Westly's head, wrapped all six legs around his skull, and tugged with little grunts. "Zug Zug give you dinner. Give you Zug Zug's dinner."

The fly was tiny, but Westly couldn't ignore his sincere efforts. In truth, Westly was scared. He didn't know where he belonged. He didn't know where he fit in. And he was certainly confused about who he was.

"Are you sure you don't want to stay with us?" the moth asked, who had waited as the other insects left.

In the distance, strange noises drifted through the mist. *Maybe being alone isn't ABSOLUTELY necessary*, Westly thought. He huffed, trying to hide his fear. "Well, if it's so important that I come along, then fine. I'll come with you—for tonight."

The moth smiled.

"Yay!" Zug Zug shouted, zipping in circles around Westly's head.

Westly followed the moth and Zug Zug into the under-growth. For the first time that day, he felt like he was taking an important step forward.

"You made the right decision, Westly," said the moth with-out looking back. "And I have a feeling you're more important than you believe yourself to be."

Westly barely heard the moth's words, already sulking over the fact that his life was not turning out the way he'd planned.

Chapter 8

All through the night they marched. The insects carried rucksacks filled with spices, herbs, and soft roots, and watertight pouches strapped around their waists. Though these pouches were sealed shut, Westly found that his sense of smell had blossomed since his change. He could smell everything around him, including the nectar inside the pouches. But it was not the exotic nectar that the butterflies drank. Rather, this nectar smelled almost like grass, or like it had come from the stem of a plant rather than the nectar bud.

All the same, it was still nectar, and the food in those packs was a meal waiting to be eaten. The night's march provided

more walking than Westly had ever experienced in his entire life. Within the first hour he was starving and exhausted.
Dreams of gentle butterfly wings festered in his mind and hurt
his heart. He clutched at his grumbling stomach frequently in
hopes that someone would at least notice and offer to stop to
eat—something, anything to distract him from the pain.

No one even seemed to notice or if they did they didn't let
on. A few of the insects grumbled about how far they had gone
off course for the rescue while looking sidelong at their new
companion.

The dragonfly neither joined in the complaints nor stopped
them, leading the group from the front. Zug Zug didn't seem
aware of anything beyond whatever plant he was currently
tormenting, and the moth simply walked in silence alongside
Westly.

Since he'd left the butterfly kingdom, Westly had been either running, falling, drowning, or nearly getting eaten. His
skin burned, his eyes were weary, and his feet made of lead. He
began to fall asleep. When he started walking off the trail, the
other insects had to shout at him to wake him up, and then
everyone had to stop while Westly hurried to catch up again.

Though Westly tried not to repeat his mistake, it wasn't
long before he was once again headed in the wrong direction.
And after the third time, the dragonfly threw Westly on a large

beetle's back, pulling the beetle's largest pack of herbs off to carry himself.

Zug Zug landed on Westly's shoulder and fell asleep instantly, buzzing softly in his ear. Frustrated and ashamed, Westly fell into a dreamy sleep in which he was tumbling down a dry streambed.

The smell of smoke touched Westly's nose and he awoke with a start. *Are we nearly home?* he wondered. *And where is home?* He had lost track of the time, but he was quite sure they had marched the entire night long. The detour to pull Westly out of the clamper, as they had called it, must have truly been a long one.

They marched down a wide slope until they came into a small valley in the grass where a hollow log lay half-buried in the earth. Candlelit windows were cut into the sides and a trail of smoke rose from a chimney. A scent of baked mushrooms, three-leaf clover, and white moss filled the air, similar enough to caterpillar food that the memories it brought back to Westly were more painful than stimulating.

But the view inside was incredible; the log was vast and filled with working insects. A few ants on crates packed small bags of the day's food into large empty crevices. The rest of the food the insects cooked over an open fire. The honeybees worked on a slate of honeycomb towards the ceiling, and beetles lifted empty crates into stacks. The inside of the log was literally abuzz with activity as the insects organized their harvest.

Westly stared in awe. The dragonfly walked up beside him and touched him on the back. Westly flipped around, startled. The dragonfly gestured to a series of nooks at the entrance that held rough blankets and pillows for sleeping.

"Oh, thank—" Westly began, but the dragonfly was already gone. Zug Zug reappeared, orbiting Westly's head, and the little fly piped, "Zug Zug food waiting. Come! Eat! Eat!"

The little fly led Westly to the fire, where the others were scooping bowls of stew out of a large kettle and slurping it down in one gulp. Then Zug Zug disappeared.

There was little left of the food from the day's collection that was not eaten immediately; only a few sacks had been set aside by the ants, presumably for storage.

As the insects around him talked, Westly listened carefully, hoping to learn more about them. They called their home Log Hallow. They usually called themselves by the name of their species such as *ant, beetle, termite,* and so on. The names were unusual to Westly because the butterflies had always lumped all of these insects together as dirt eaters.

He saw all the insects working at tasks fit for their species—whether it was leaping, carrying, squeezing, or crushing. Westly was particularly fascinated when he saw a grasshopper leap through the sky, wings fluttering, to deliver a message to a nearby beetle.

The smell of the stew eventually attracted his attention and he found himself staring into the pot. It looked extraordinarily delicious; it came close to caterpillar standards. Westly's stomach burbled again and, seeing the small amount of food disappearing so quickly, he hurriedly reached for a stack of bowls lying nearby.

All the insects suddenly stopped eating, their heads turning toward him. Wondering what he'd done, Westly staggered backward.

The centipede who had yelled at Westly earlier that day growled, "No work, no food." Then all resumed sucking down the stew as fast as they could.

As Westly fell back onto a piece of bark, he noticed for the first time the cold breeze coming from the foggy air. He shivered and rubbed his arms as he looked around.

"Zug Zug food here!" a high voice called. The little fly

zipped into Westly's face, spilling a cup of brown sticky goo all over Westly's lap.

The smell of Zug Zug's food was not quite as good as the other insects', but it was welcome anyway, and Westly's stomach grumbled again.

The fly smiled widely at Westly, plopped the cup on his wet legs, and waited.

The urge to eat was overpowering. Westly yanked the cup to his lips, lifted it high in the air, and slurped it down in one motion.

The fly squealed with excitement and buzzed in circles.

Even when it was gone Westly continued licking the rest out of the cup and off his fingers. When those were clean, he looked to see if there was any more, still quite hungry. But all Westly saw was the dragonfly watching him at a distance.

Concluding that there would, sadly, be no more food that night, Westly felt a wave of sleep break quickly over him. He staggered to his feet and walked wearily towards his new bed. As he bent down, a hand clamped on his shoulder and spun him around.

It was the dragonfly, his stern face close to Westly's. "No time for sleep tonight. Work always starts with the light of the fog." He pointed out the door.

If there was any sign of the fog growing lighter, Westly could not see it.

"No sleep?" Westly asked weakly.

The dragonfly gave him a long stare before flitting away.

Westly couldn't believe it. Butterflies slept in as long as they wanted every day—caterpillars especially. He had never been up before the sunrise in his whole life. But apparently all the other insects instinctively recognized the lighting of the fog, for as they finished gobbling down their bowls of stew they immediately made their way back to the rucksacks.

Had he still been a prince, Westly would simply have told the others to go on without him and claimed that he had official business without telling anyone what it was. That's what his father would have done, anyway, and few in the butterfly kingdom would have minded if they found out Westly had simply gone back to bed.

The realization that those royal perks were gone forever shook Westly to his core. He wasn't sure he was willing to fall in line with these creatures. His instinct was to simply thank them for their help and leave. But he knew he would feel guilty if he did. Their kindness was something that he did not want to lose. He was in their debt. If he was going to repay them he had no choice but to follow them without a moment's hesitation. And so he ran to catch up to them.

It was not a long march to their destination, a large mud pit surrounded by overhanging ferns and nettles. It smelled of mildew and weeds, and Westly thought it might make a creature sick to step in it. The fog was indeed a little lighter now. Though it wasn't overly bright, somehow the intensity of the whiteness hurt Westly's eyes. He had to blink constantly and rub at them.

As the insects put their rucksacks down on the side of the clearing and looked it over, the dragonfly landed on a fern directly overhead and hung upside down, amazing Westly. The maneuver was smooth, artistic, and commanding—like a warrior from the butterfly legends. Having been a caterpillar all his life, Westly found the sensation of being in awe of a dirt eater—of all creatures—to be wholly unexpected, perhaps even a bit unwelcome.

"All right, everyone. We have to make up for the lost harvest yesterday—you all saw how bare the cupboards are. Keep your heads up and watch out; fliers will be working double speed. If we can finish this before the fog dims we'll hit the raspberry patch on the way back."

Westly had never heard of raspberries. From what the dragonfly had said, it sounded like they were supposed to be a reward. But the insects gave no outward sign of excitement, so Westly decided he must have been wrong.

There were several ants in the group, and as far as Westly could tell they never spoke out loud. Instead, it was as though they read each other's minds. As soon as the dragonfly finished speaking they made their way slowly but surely through the mud and climbed onto the mushrooms in the center. With their scrawny legs they latched onto one of the smaller mushroom heads and began to squeeze.

It baffled Westly. They looked like they were trying to give the mushroom a hug. Cute, but pointless. When a grasshopper bounded overhead, Westly lost interest and turned to follow it instead.

This long green insect delivered messages to the beetles around the clearing, telling them where they should wait to pick up their loads. The grasshopper's giant leaps here in the open air fascinated Westly; it reached heights of at least two, sometimes three feet—perhaps even more. It looked like an awful lot of fun. Westly was tempted to ask the creature for a ride.

Now wasn't the right time for it, but the thought gave Westly an idea.

"Excuse me," Westly said, running back to the dragonfly. "Excuse me!"

The leader was talking to a praying mantis, and he turned rather sharply at being interrupted. "How may I help you?"

"I was wondering if I might be able to help the grasshopper deliver messages."

"What good would you be able to do that he cannot already do?"

"Good? Oh. Right. Um, he must get out of breath, jumping around like that, right? So that means it's hard for him to speak. I'll ride on his back and relay the instructions."

The dragonfly gave him a deadpan stare. "No."

"No? But that's what I want to do."

"He's fine on his own, and we'll need you elsewhere, I'm sure. Please wait and I'll be with you shortly."

After the dragonfly turned away, Westly bit his tongue and wandered off a few feet.

While Westly had talked with the dragonfly, the ants' efforts were revealed: their squeezing had shattered the mushroom head into a dozen pieces. The flying beetles carefully and slowly picked the pieces out of the mud and hefted them to the side, where termites and crickets stowed the food into rucksacks.

Westly decided that if he was going to be in the clearing all day, he would find something that *he* felt was worth doing, whether the dragonfly wanted it or not. Whistling softly, he meandered around the clearing, observing the process and thinking.

The first opportunity he spotted was a patch of unfamiliar flowers hanging at the border of the clearing. The insects
apparently hadn't noticed that within the flowers there were
clearly buds of nectar. As they would no doubt be thirsty soon,
Westly had the perfect solution.

He climbed on the back of a beetle and then leapt to the
nearest petal. When his foot touched the inside of the flower,
the pollen turned out to be looser than any he had ever experienced on the chandelier. With one step the pollen poofed
wildly into the air. The more Westly moved, the thicker the air
became, and soon a plume of powder was pouring downward,
filling Westly's lungs and nostrils. With a giant sneeze, Westly
blew himself right out of the flower and landed in the mud.

Opening his eyes, he saw that the pollen had covered not
only himself, but also all the bugs that happened to be nearby
the flower. They were all hacking and coughing away. Before
anyone could notice who had agitated the flowers, Westly
sneaked into the bushes.

As he looked around this time, he saw a large beetle holding a chunk of mushroom so big that he was unable to see.
Westly hurried out in front of the beetle and began trying to
direct it, calling, "This way . . . this way."

Everything worked perfectly at first. The beetle seemed to
be obeying him, and the two safely approached the growing

mound of food. But as Westly walked backward, he was caught unawares and stepped in front of another beetle who was also blinded by a large chunk of mushroom. When it ran into Westly it dropped the mushroom right on top of him. As if on cue, Westly's beetle dropped his food on top of him too. And then a third, and a fourth. By the time Westly finally managed to free himself from the growing pile, he was red in the face with bruises.

As Westly sat panting and wiping away the mushroom flecks it occurred to him that perhaps now would be a good time to go ask the dragonfly for specific instructions. But he refused to be a mindless servant—that kind of behavior was for commoners. He was of a royal butterfly bloodline.

His mind searched frantically for another idea, and suddenly it came to him what he should do. He ran through the trail of beetles, climbed past the flowers, leapt to the stem of a fern, and scurried up its branch until he reached the tip. There he pulled out something about which he had entirely forgotten until now: his thread.

Sitting on the tip of the fern he looked down to see that it hung perfectly over the mushroom patch in the mud. Smiling to himself, he attached the end of the thread to the stem of a nearby leaf.

Westly plucked the thread—*twang!*—to make sure it was

secure. Then he dropped off the fern and inched his way down to the pile of broken crumbs. When he landed he glanced around to make sure no one was watching and then quickly pulled his thread as tight as it would go. High above, the fern bent towards him and excitement filled Westly's stomach as he thought about how impressed they would be to see his cleverness.

Zug Zug saw what Westly was doing and exuberantly zipped over and hovered near Westly's head to watch.

Westly bent down and stuck the end of the thread onto the top of an extremely heavy mushroom head, one even larger than a beetle could lift. The mushroom stretched upward, its stem getting thinner and taut. Once more Westly looked around to make sure his surprise was still a secret, grinned to himself, and fixed his eyes on the pile of rucksacks across the clearing. *Now, if my calculations are correct, all I need to do is cut this stem and . . .*

Westly climbed onto the mushroom and, bending under the cap, raised his arm high in the air. Zug Zug, buzzing excitedly around Westly's head, followed suit. His eyes pinched shut, Westly brought his sharp hand down and cut through the mushroom stem.

The mushroom cap ripped upwards and zoomed through the air. Westly's smile broadened into an open-mouthed grin as the wind hit his face, Zug Zug clinging onto the back of his head for the ride of his life.

The edge of the clearing drew nearer. All the insects were still ignorant of what was about to land right among them.

Westly opened his mouth, getting ready to bite the thread as soon as the mushroom head had reached the right spot.

Far above Westly's head, a beetle hummed to himself as he flew casually through the air carrying a load of food, completely unaware of Westly's thread swinging up behind him. The thread slammed into the beetle's back, sticking right between his wings, and he cried out in surprise as the thread yanked him along.

Westly, just about ready to bite through the thread and finish his glorious plan, felt a giant jolt from above instead. The thread bounced hard and Westly barely managed to hold onto the mushroom cap as he and Zug Zug swung violently upwards and then began zooming back in the opposite direction.

Their new direction found them aiming straight at the ants, still standing on the mushrooms and only just having noticed Westly and Zug Zug streaking toward them.

The dragonfly, who all this time had been busily instructing a group of katydids in their duties, just barely caught a glimpse of a mushroom cap swinging across the field.

POW! Westly's mushroom cap pendulum smacked all of the ants clean away. They tumbled into the underbrush.

The dragonfly's face grew hot with anger as he watched Westly twirling onwards, hanging onto the mushroom cap for dear life. "What is that creature doing?" the dragonfly shouted as he flew into the air, waving at a dozen other insects to follow.

High above, another beetle came to rescue the first, still spinning around in the sticky string. Both beetles tugged and twisted at the thread, trying to break him free. Then, with a gigantic *twang!* the thread snapped in two.

Down and down the beetles tumbled toward the clearing and, just as the dragonfly and his recruits reached Westly's mushroom, the beetles bashed into the rescue party.

Wings and feet flew in all directions, getting tangled every which way in Westly's sticky string. Any insects fortunate enough to not be wrapped up stood in awe, motionless.

Westly landed (unluckily) on his back but (luckily) on a soft pile of leaves. The mushroom cap then landed (unluckily again) right on top of him. Stuck in the porous mushroom cap, Westly had to chew his way upwards until his head popped out of its bready flesh.

The whole clan stared at him in wonder.

Westly gave a weak smile, mushroom flecks stuck in his teeth, and Zug Zug bounced proudly on his head.

Chapter 9

"Considering the circumstances, perhaps it would be best if I left for a little while?" Westly asked meekly.

Everyone glared at him.

"Right . . . That would be a yes," Westly added as he scrambled out of the mushroom cap.

Shamefaced and without offering any sort of explanation he skittered out of the muddy clearing and into the thick underbrush. As the sound of insects arguing faded into the distance, Westly felt a wave of depression flow from his head to his eight pointed feet.

"Great," he murmured to himself. "First I let down my family, and now I let down these dirt eaters. It's no wonder nobody wants me. I don't seem to belong anywhere. I'm pathetic."

Rap-tap-tap! A loud noise boomed behind Westly. He spun around, thinking he'd somehow triggered another dangerous plant.

Outside the glass windows of the menagerie was a creature so large it dwarfed any insect Westly had ever seen in his life by more than a hundred times. The light shining behind the creature clearly outlined its broad shoulders, thin feet, clawed toes, and long pointed nose—or was that a mouth? The creature was smiling in a way that made it look like his feathered face, deep-seated eyes, and bony mouth was almost a mask—the kind a butterfly might wear to a ball.

But what this creature was wearing struck Westly most of all. He wore multiple layers: jackets, frills, pantaloons, vests, and more. Jewelry covered much of his body and a wide flared collar came up around his neckline, spreading out dramatically to surround his skull. His clothing was so thick Westly thought it a wonder he could even stand.

The creature was terribly frightening. He cocked his head to the side, and then pointed with a long, feathery finger northward.

Westly turned to look in that direction, but what little might be seen through the fog was blocked by the undergrowth. He turned back to stare at the creature again, but he was gone.

Was this giant feathered creature the same thing he'd seen the night before the changing ceremony? He spun around to see if anyone else had noticed it, but the other insects were too far away.

Grateful for the distraction, Westly decided to go exploring and find out what all this meant. The leaves grew thick as he trudged into the brush. For a while, Westly kept one hand on the glass wall to keep from getting lost. However, he soon came to a place where vines and dirt completely covered his one source of direction and he had no choice but to wander blindly. Not long after he let go of the wall he saw something he had not seen in two days—pure sunlight.

He climbed up to where the streak of light landed on a high leaf and found that it was in the shape of a keyhole. Glancing up, he saw the small square wooden door to which

the keyhole belonged. The light behind the door flickered for a moment, went dark altogether, and then returned again suddenly.

Was the creature moving behind the door?

Westly crawled carefully through a tangle of vines and nervously took his first glance outside. It was the first time he had ever seen the land surrounding the menagerie, as the butterflies in the atrium could only see the sky.

The land itself held only a dead orchard. The tall black feathery creature stood on a branch of one of the smaller trees.

Westly licked his lips and tapped his hands together. While he had always known there was a world outside the menagerie, it had never occurred to Westly that he would ever see it, let alone explore it. Though wandering into this new world excited Westly to no end, there was another feeling that told him to wait. He remembered the butterfly legends about the insects who had established this little home within glass. The legends said that the creatures outside were unpredictable—they lived by a different set of rules.

Despite the voice in Westly's head telling him to turn and run, this new creature seemed friendly. His long mouth appeared to be smiling. And judging by his clothing, it looked as though he bore the same love of finery as the butterflies—perhaps even more. Still, something didn't feel right. Instinctively Westly turned and stepped back into the menagerie.

The sunlight coming through the hole suddenly disappeared and it caused Westly to turn and see what had eclipsed the sun.

A giant eye peered into the keyhole.

"I can help you," the creature said in a thin voice.

Westly's jaw dropped open. The eye was enormous—twice the size of his little body. The eye stared back at him.

Westly licked his lips and stammered, "Who—who are you? What do you want?"

"Do you want my name? Or the kind of creature I am?"

Westly didn't answer.

A gentle chuckle came from the opposite side of the door. "No need to fear me. I'm not here to harm you."

The creature took a few steps backward and said with a deep bow, "I am the raven. That is what others call me." Then with a smile he said, "May I ask your name, little spider?"

"Spider?"

The raven stood upright. "Don't tell me you've forgotten the name of your species?"

"Species?"

"Oh dear. Are you truly this naive?"

Westly began to shake his head in protest, but something occurred to him. This raven was the first creature to recognize Westly not as an unnamed insect, nor a mutated butterfly, but something he could describe, something apparently normal. The thought, both intriguing and perplexing, kept Westly from speaking.

"Well, you are in greater need than I thought," said the raven. "Yes, indeed, you are a spider, Mister . . . ?"

Westly only eyed him suspiciously.

The raven sighed. "I can see you don't trust me, and I suppose if I were in your shoes I might feel the same. But I do hope our difference in size won't stand between us—as friends. Can't you trust me?"

Westly took a few slow steps closer to the keyhole until he was sitting just below it.

"I'm merely interested in coming to know the story of this nest of glass," the raven continued. "It must have been a long time since any of you had contact with the outside world, and I've traveled far to find such a place. You see, I like to collect things, stories being among my most favorite collectables. And stories of long lost insects are perhaps the most collectable of all."

Westly climbed up and poked his head out of the keyhole to listen more closely.

"Of course, in your particular case, I think I already read most of your story in your eyes."

"How do you mean?"

"Well, you obviously find yourself unwelcome within that group of insects; otherwise you wouldn't have wandered away without them saying anything or coming after you. And you're completely out of your element, so you're looking for adventure. What is most extraordinary, I believe, is that you have no idea of your remarkable capabilities. And so, considering all these facts, how could you possibly know who you truly are?"

Westly tilted his head to the side. "I'm sorry—I don't understand what it is that you want from me."

"*Want?* Well, nothing more than a friend . . . and perhaps a few good laughs together," the raven replied. As he spoke, he pulled a long thin string from within his robes that he began twisting back and forth through his fingers in a complicated pattern. "When I saw you through that window, I thought that perhaps you could use a pointer or two about how to make yourself useful—even respectable—amongst the other insects.

Hmm? You see, I've seen
spiders like you before,
and I know a thing or
two about what you can
do, especially with that
thread that caused so much
trouble a moment ago."

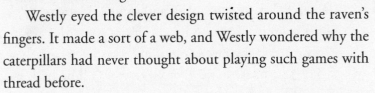

Westly eyed the clever design twisted around the raven's
fingers. It made a sort of a web, and Westly wondered why the
caterpillars had never thought about playing such games with
thread before.

"There are many more patterns that I know, but that's only
the beginning of what you can do," the raven continued, "if
you'll let me teach you. You're capable of much more than you
realize."

Westly retreated slowly back into the keyhole. Despite the
raven's kind words, Westly still felt uneasy. He could not tell
if it was simply because the creature was so unusually large, or
because he worried about communicating with outsiders, or
because of the old stories.

Perhaps the ancestors had been wrong about outsiders, he
mused. Or maybe the true history of the menagerie was forgotten. Indeed, Westly had climbed just beyond the edge of
the keyhole and the raven had done nothing to him.

Biting his lip, Westly paused for a moment, and decided to try a test. "No, thank you," he replied.

"'No, thank you'?"

Westly waited to see what the raven would do. Would he get angry, or prideful, or something else?

The raven gave Westly a long glance out of the corner of his eye, and Westly nearly ran right then and there.

But the raven sniffed finally and sighed. "Very well, suit yourself. I promise I had no idea to harm you. All I wanted was a friend," said the raven, spreading wide his strange black wings. Then he paused and glanced down. "I'll be back here tomorrow morning, should you change your mind. I do hope that you will; I'm so lonely on this island all by myself. Well, toot-a-loo."

Before Westly could say anything more, the raven gave a loud flap of his wings and was gone.

Chapter 10

We root 'em out, and they keep comin' back. Those carnivorous plants'll eat a bug faster than he can beat a wing," the centipede growled, leaning in low over the kettle.

The young grubs crept closer, their shadows growing tall on the walls of their log home.

Westly, who was sitting by the moth, the beetle, and the mantis, also felt a bit frightened—not from the story, but rather from the memory of his own encounter.

"So you know what we do?" the centipede continued. "We feed 'em poisoned herbs. Confuse 'em. Pick out things like hemlock, spurges, and baneberry—make 'em think they's eatin' bug blood. The poison don't affect 'em—they's already made of venom enough. But it fills 'em up, and sometimes you get lucky and they just spits ya back out."

"What happens if it doesn't?" asked a wide-eyed child. The storyteller squinted.

"You don't get lucky."

All the children gasped.

"But, they ain't nothin' compared to what they'll do to themselves . . . Those weeds out there—nettles an' milkweed an' stuff—they'll twist the roots right off a vine, make it die within a week—if we don't find it first. See, it's like there's a whole war inside the menagerie: they's fightin' us, an' we's fightin' them, and they's fightin' themselves, like stirred-up hover-flies."

"I never knew," Westly whispered, keeping his head down. He had a bowl of stew in his hands—the moth had given it to Westly for making an effort, but Westly hadn't touched it. "You've been fighting those plants back down here for how long?" Westly asked.

Without looking at Westly, the centipede huffed, "We been fightin' maybe two, three years now to keep 'em down. But if they ever make it up those vines, they'll rot the tree canopy right out, an' the trees'll be as dead as that cursed well—"

"—Why aren't there any regular flowers down here?" Westly blurted, then bit his tongue.

"You sure seem to know a lot about this place for a creature that just hatched," replied the centipede.

Westly bit his lip, and shrugged. "Instinct?"

"Stinks?" Zug Zug said, only halfway listening to the

conversation. "Oooh, me likes stinks. Me thinks food stinks is good good."

"Hmph," the centipede murmured. "Well, flowers only grow where there's sunshine—an' we ain't got none of that. 'Sides, they's just pretty. And there ain't much worth in looks."

"Yes there is," Westly protested. "Why don't we try it? I bet it would be beautiful."

"You sure you ain't met a fuzzhead already?" asked the centipede.

"Fuzzhead?" Westly asked. He'd heard the term somewhere lately, but didn't know what it meant. The centipede huffed. "You know . . . wingers—"

"—Fraggers," the mantis said.

"—Gnat brains," the beetle said.

Westly only grew more puzzled.

"Butterflies," the moth murmured, staring into the fire.

"Oh," Westly whispered and shrank back in his seat. "No. But so what if I had? Is there something wrong with them?"

"So what? So you'd be associatin' with a buncha lazy pond scum. We keep those vine roots free, make the air nice and clear, and till up the whole forest. Those nutters up there? Don't even know how to say thank you. Just look down their curly-cue noses at us."

"And that's fine with us," said the mantis. "We keep the

kids away from them. Let them grow up the right way—working for a living."

The beetle nodded silently.

"'Sides, if they was to come down here," the centipede continued, "they'd get chewed up and torn to pieces by what's down here. Last less than a day, I tell you."

Westly glanced around at all the grubs sitting by their parents. They looked terrified. He whispered to the mantis, "Shouldn't we be talking about this later—you know, after the kids are asleep?"

The mantis blinked. "Why?"

"I just . . . you know, thought it might give them nightmares or something."

"Shoot," scoffed the centipede, who overheard.

And the mantis shook his head. "It's their world too. They gotta live in it, so they gotta know what it's like—unless you want 'em to die."

"No, no, of course not," Westly answered.

"Who're you to talk, anyhow?" the centipede spat. "With all that trouble you caused today? Coulda killed us all."

Westly bit his lip.

"Leave him alone," the mantis said. "He's new around here. He'll get his act together, won't ya, Wes?"

Westly nodded quickly.

"New? I don't know about that," the centipede mumbled. "He knows twice as much as I knew when I hatched. How's that?"

"You're gonna have to pick a higher standard," the mantis replied with a grin.

Before the conversation could go any further, Westly stood and walked away.

It was odd that it was here among the dirt eaters that Westly had learned the butterfly kingdom was not as independent as they believed. The forest, the clean air, probably even the water from the sprinklers: it was all kept clean by the gardeners. If it wasn't for them, the kingdom would be overrun with weeds and uninhabitable.

He heard footsteps not far away and jumped. When his eyes adjusted to the light he saw that it was only the dragonfly, busy sorting the empty rucksacks.

Westly's thoughts about the butterfly kingdom disappeared, replaced by the rotten memory of what had happened earlier in the day. He walked over to the dragonfly and tapped him on the shoulder.

The tall creature turned, saw who it was, and then returned to organizing. "How can I help you, Westly?"

Wishing the dragonfly would turn and face him, Westly stammered, "Listen, I'm—I'm sorry about today—"

"It's fine. Don't mention it," the dragonfly said, his voice showing no emotion. "We eat hand to mouth, in case you haven't noticed, and there's no time for living in the past. Tomorrow you'll find a way to make up for it, I'm sure."

After waiting for the dragonfly to say anything else, Westly finally took a few backward steps and then walked into the darkness.

For a short while he walked in the opposite direction of Log Hallow. He wanted to get away and never see it again, to just disappear into the trees. But still, the thought of letting down yet another group was worse. He needed to prove to himself that he could be valuable to someone, somewhere— even if it was in just this one small place.

How, though? What he'd done earlier in the day was an utter disaster. And there would be no honor in doing some lowly task for the dragonfly. It had to be something unique.

What the raven had said came back to him. "You're capable of much more than you realize." What had the raven meant by that? There was only one way to find out, and so off into the fog Westly went.

It did not take long to find his way back to the vine-covered doorway. Just as a hint of light grew at the horizon, Westly was at the keyhole.

"Mr. Raven?" Westly whispered. "Mr. Raven?"

Carefully, Westly squeezed through the keyhole and used his thread to rappel down the door until he reached the grass on the other side. He crawled through a group of dry, unfamiliar weeds and under the dead trees. After a long hike, Westly arrived at the foot of a black stream that ran into the ocean. Westly stared at the watery horizon as if he were spellbound. He had never seen so much water. It was the most beautiful thing he had ever seen.

Behind Westly, in the shadows of the dead orchard, a shadow moved. As it fell upon him, he spun around to find he was cowering at the feet of the gigantic raven—who smiled brightly at his small black friend.

Westly gulped. He could not believe what he was doing.

"I *am* glad to see you, my little spider," the raven said. "How kind of you to come so far—and all for me."

"H-Hello, Mr. Raven. I—you—you said you could help me," Westly replied. "W-Well, h-h-here I am."

The raven breathed in through his nostrils and grinned.

Though Westly was trying his best not to show it, this was the most terrifying moment he had ever experienced.

The raven suddenly slapped his feathered wing across his forehead, and his face grew somber. "Oh, dear me! Where are my manners? Why, you must be terrified out here! First time in all your life leaving that glass cage. Here, here. Come, sit down on this rock and have a drop of nectar. I'll bet you've never tasted anything like it." He plucked a bottle from within his robes, opened it with a snap, and twirled it to the ground in front of Westly.

When the raven had retreated a few feet from the rock, Westly politely put his hand into the bottle, extracted a few drops, and sat down, sucking softly on his trembling fingers. The taste of it was exquisite.

"There, that's right. Cool your nerves," soothed the raven as he took a perch high on a rock opposite Westly.

They sat in silence for a minute while Westly licked his fingers. On the ground near the raven, he noticed a pile of odds and ends—bowls, little glass jars, and other shiny trinkets.

The raven noticed him looking, and smiled and winked. "Oh, don't mind those. I collect things. That's what I do."

Westly felt his heart slow its hammering as the raven continued. "Well, it's only been a day, and we've already come a long way in our friendship. But really, in a way we're also still right where we started: you know my name but I do not know yours."

"My name? Oh! My name . . ." Westly said, sitting up straight. "I'm Westly."

"*Westly!* That's an extraordinary name. Westly, whom I met at the wall. What an unlikely relationship, you and I. Only fate would have it," the raven remarked. "Tell me, Westly, what's it like inside that glass nest of yours? I've only caught a glimpse or two from the outside. Is it so cloudy all the way through? And why do those creatures at the bottom choose to stay down there in the dark? Why not go up where the beautiful butterflies are?"

While the raven continued chattering as nonchalant as could be, Westly began to believe that he was indeed right in coming here. If this giant creature had meant to harm him, he would have done so by now.

"Inside the menagerie?" Westly repeated, and then looked at the surrounding orchard. "Well . . . it's really kind of boring in there, I suppose. Not like out here." Westly lifted up his nectar bottle to illustrate. "There's some nectar up top, and it's pretty good. I'm not sure if it's as good as this, though. I've kind of forgotten. But the gardeners don't—we don't really get to drink it. Just the butterflies."

"The gardeners?"

"Yeah. They're the bugs who live in the fog—everyone but the butterflies, actually. I used to think the gardeners were scary before . . . when I was . . . But they're really nice, too— most of them, at least."

The raven scrutinized him.

"Anyway, yeah. The butterflies live at the top, and we stay at the bottom."

"An odd juxtaposition. Why, I would think that if your friends are any bit as brave as you, they wouldn't hesitate to live wherever they like."

Westly shrugged. "It's just the way it is. They're convinced that the butterflies are too rude and obsessed with themselves 'cause they're so pretty and all."

"Ahh—jealousy," the raven said with a nod. "Amazing how the vices invade even the most secluded fortresses."

"They're jealous?"

"Of course! Just because you don't have an envy for beauty does not mean that the others do not also."

"What do you mean?"

"Well, you've seen them, your gardeners. They don't have the looks of the butterflies, and it can't be easy gazing up all the time, if you see what I mean."

"I didn't realize," said Westly, making sense of it. Of course—Westly still wanted to live among the butterflies, but was ashamed because he was ugly. It must be the same with all the other bugs.

"You are but a child," the raven said, and stroked Westly's head with one long feather. "Furthermore, you've never seen anything else. 'A fish born in a filthy pond knows nothing of fresh water.' But stick with me, and I will show you the way. It's the tall who see the small most clearly."

At the word *child*, Westly bristled again; it reminded him of why he had come. With a glance he noticed that the dim light at the horizon was growing. The others would not sleep much longer, and they would notice Westly's absence.

"You said earlier that I'm a spider?" Westly said. "You've heard of my kind?"

"Oh, yes. Quite. Does this mean that you are alone? You have no family?"

Westly nodded.

"Curious. I wonder how you ever got here. But no matter. What's important is that you're here now, and you've come with a set of talents unlike any other creature in the world."

Westly's heart swelled. "So you'll show me what those are? You'll show me that trick you did—the one with your hands? And what it's good for?"

The raven laughed. "Of course—and much more. But first, we begin at the beginning. There. Sit still . . . good. Now pull out some thread, take your hand, and put one corner over the other . . ."

Chapter 11

S ee, it's called a web," Westly explained, pulling over as many creatures as he could to watch his demonstration. "So, if I hold four hands like this . . . and then pull out an inch or so of thread . . . and then . . . I think I go like this . . ." he explained, weaving as best as he could remember.

As the pattern grew more and more complicated, the other insects rubbed their noses and glanced awkwardly at the mint-leaf field they were supposed to be harvesting.

"I've almost got it. All I have to do is, uh, well . . . there! See?" Westly held his hands up. Stretched between them was a tangled mess of thread and spider glue. Westly tapped his chin thoughtfully and didn't notice that the sticky thread had stuck to his face. "It worked a lot better when I did it this morning."

"Sure," the centipede growled, plopping an acorn helmet on his head and scooting away. With a kind nod a fat beetle countered, "I'm sure it did, Westly. We believe you." Then he yawned and left as well.

The little crowd dispersed quickly, leaving Westly by himself at the side of the field.

He began trying to untangle his fingers, glancing occasionally at the others as they worked.

Harvesting the mint field was a grueling task. The insects had to bite away the stem of each mint leaf, lower it to the ground, and then work together in teams to move it through the heavy brush. When they finally reached the side of the field the ants cut it to pieces and sorted it into the rucksacks.

"All right, it's your turn now," the dragonfly said from behind Westly.

Westly, startled, spun around, the thread that hung from his chin slapping the tall creature's nose.

"I-I'm sorry, Mr. Dragonfly," Westly stammered, yanking the thread back.

"It's okay, Westly." The dragonfly sighed heavily and looked at a map sketched on a dry leaf. "I know you want to help but I'm not sure what to have you do. What are you good at?"

"Well . . ." Westly held up the thread. "Maybe I could do something with this."

The dragonfly looked at the wad of snarled thread on his fingers.

Westly dropped his hand. "I just need to practice a little."

"Unfortunately, there isn't time to practice hobbies. There's a lot of work to be done," said the dragonfly. "And we need everyone to help. But we need you to do something . . . useful. Do you understand?"

Westly hung his head and nodded.

"Good." The dragonfly looked him over again. "Hmm. I believe you'd be a great weed hunter."

"Weeds?" replied Westly.

"Yes, weeds. Milkweed specifically. It's infested the southern end of the patch. The grasshoppers can handle lifting it out, but they're not the best at hunting it down. They get a little distracted."

Westly raised an eyebrow.

The dragonfly pointed back over Westly's shoulder to a dozen grasshoppers who were gobbling down the very mint leaf they were supposed to be harvesting.

The dragonfly sighed, "I'd better get over there. Can you help with the weeds? Just go through the field, mark the weeds with sticks wherever you find them, and I'll get the grasshoppers to follow behind."

Westly felt a surge of belonging. He liked having a job to do. "Okay," he said, turning to obey.

The mint leaf patch was a lot larger than Westly had realized and the milkweeds were well hidden. The work was hard and took his full attention. In no time the sounds of the others faded away.

Westly had been working for some time when he heard a familiar buzzing sound. He turned and found Zug Zug the happy little fly darting around him. The happiness he'd felt earlier from being included had faded with work, leaving him tired and grumpy. "Zug Zug, I'm not in the mood."

The little fly kept zipping happily around Westly's head. He tried to swat at him but only succeeded in making Zug Zug think they were playing a game.

"Patty-cake!" Zug Zug yelled. He knocked himself against Westly's hands over and over again, singing, "Patty-cake! Patty-cake!"

"You're impossible," Westly moaned and trudged onward.

More time passed as Westly crawled under the mint plants looking for early milkweed sprouts and marked them with twigs. As time went on, it became less and less fun. Westly began to grumble. Why couldn't he have a job that wasn't so hard? As the ruler of the butterflies, he wouldn't have had to work like this! Life wasn't fair!

Grumbling helped to pass the time, but it didn't make him feel any better. If anything, he began to feel worse.

After a while he sat down, pulled out a length of thread,

and tried to figure out the pattern that the raven had shown him, but he couldn't keep it from tangling around his fingers.

Frustrated, Westly tossed the snarled mess on the ground and stomped away grumbling, the thread trailing behind him.

The little fly stopped to investigate the sticky threads and realized to his delight that if he untangled the knots, he could stick the thread to the surrounding leaves. So as Westly walked, Zug Zug followed behind, sticking the thread to anything he could reach.

Westly didn't realize what was happening until he heard the grasshoppers coming up behind him and turned to make sure his sticks were visible. Westly's jaw dropped.

The leaves behind him were all tied together. He caught sight of Zug Zug as he darted around the mint leaves, wrapping sticky threads around everything, whistling happily to himself.

"No!" Westly shouted, pulling his hands down his face. "Zug Zug, if anyone stumbles into this, it'll be another disaster—just like yesterday."

Zug Zug gave Westly a puzzled look.

"Gah!" Westly raged. "We've got to get this cleaned up—*now!*" He grabbed at the nearest sticky threads.

In the distance a grasshopper bounded into view, then disappeared into the mint leaves, only to leap again, this time a bit closer. Another grasshopper followed, and then another, and finally the buzzing of the dragonfly's wings behind them.

This is going to be a disaster, Westly thought. He yanked on his cheeks and walked in circles. Once the dragonfly saw this mess he would think Westly was too dangerous to have in their group, and he'd be sent away.

There wasn't time to run around cleaning up the mess. He would just have to do what he could and hope for the best. Wrapping four hands around the thread and digging the other four legs into the dirt, Westly gave one giant yank, hoping to pull all the threads free at once.

But the threads didn't let go. They were still stuck fast to the leaves. Westly pulled harder. With a snap, a leaf broke off its stem. Then another and another.

Soon there was a whole pile of leaves lying on the ground, all connected by Westly's thread.

"What's going on here?" The dragonfly landed a little way away from Westly, a dozen grasshoppers right behind.

Westly spun around.

"Oh, I was just . . . doing what you said. Marking the weeds?"

"But what is all this?" the dragonfly asked as he pointed at the pile of mint leaves. He didn't look angry, but he didn't look pleased either. Bending to the ground, he rubbed his hands in the soil until they were safely covered with dirt, and then he reached down and took hold of the thread.

Westly winced, "Wait! Don't touch that! It's—"

The dragonfly yanked on the thread and a dozen leaves moved together, all connected.

"—sticky." Westly finished lamely.

"Yes, I can see that," the dragonfly said as he stared at the pile thoughtfully. "You did this?" he asked.

Westly slumped down, making himself as small as he possibly could. He had no idea where he was going to go after they kicked him out. "Well, I, no, um, yes, but . . ."

The dragonfly reached over and patted Westly on the head. "Good work, young man. Now I see what you were up to yesterday. This is brilliant!" And he yelled to the grasshoppers, "Come see this!"

"Wait—what?" Westly asked as he straightened back up.

The dragonfly grabbed the end of the thread and flew off, the tangled leaves trailing along behind him. The grasshoppers nodded in appreciation and followed after.

Westly's mouth dropped open as he watched them move away. Then slowly, a smile spread across his face, as he realized what had just happened. By sticking the leaves together and pulling them from the stems, he's saved them hours of work. Well, Zug Zug had. But it had been his thread that had made the difference! With a big smile, Westley turned and gave Zug Zug a pat on the head, just as the dragonfly had done for him.

The little fly took it as another game of patty-cake.

Chapter 12

The next morning, Westly and Zug Zug spent their time in the mint field, tearing off leaves and handing them to the bugs with wings while others went around marking the pesky milkweeds.

At lunch he climbed an old rotting tree with the ants and used his sticky thread to help peel away the rotting bark. In the afternoon he and the beetles lowered walnuts from the very tops of the trees. As he worked, at one point he thought he saw the colorful wings of a butterfly, but he passed it off as fluttering leaves instead. No butterfly had ever come to this part of the menagerie. He couldn't imagine them starting now, even though a small part of him hoped that someone would come looking for him.

As the soft shadows of the evening spread across the ground and the insects made their way back to Log Hallow, Westly's eight little legs were sore from work, but his heart felt full. For the first time in his life he felt useful, like he belonged. Not even Zug Zug's constant buzzing could irritate him. Westly was happy.

After dinner, he slipped away and carefully made his way to the keyhole. He didn't know if his strange friend would be waiting for him, but he hoped so. He had so much to tell him.

The trees in the orchard looked as if they'd been bathed in silver, reflecting the moonlight. A light breeze tugged at their branches, and they made a wonderful noise as they brushed against each other. The air smelled different outside the menagerie. For a moment, Westly felt a twinge of fear. With only a couple of legs outside the keyhole, he froze, unwilling to climb all the way out.

A dark shadow fluttered nearby. Westly drew his legs back in. He had decided to turn around and go back but a voice in the night stopped him.

"Ah, my dear little Westly, what brings you out after dark?"

Westly blinked a few times then relaxed as the figure emerged out of the darkness. Black wings decorated with bits and baubles shone in the moonlight. A pair of familiar red eyes blinked at him. It was the raven.

Westly sighed and pulled himself all the way out of the keyhole. "Mr. Raven. I wasn't sure if you'd be here, but I'm glad you are. I used my web today to help the other insects. I harvested leaves and pulled down nuts!" He paused to take an excited breath.

The raven chuckled. "My goodness. You must have had a good day. Take a moment and start again. I want to hear all of it. Every detail."

Westly smiled and started again, this time he didn't leave anything out. The raven oohed and aahed and praised him for his quick thinking. And when he finished, the raven was smiling.

"Well, it certainly sounds like you're learning to use your talents. I'm sure the other insects are happy to have you there."

Westly nodded. "But I want to learn more, Mr. Raven. Can you teach me?" He tried to make a web but only succeeded in tangling it. "I know I could do so much more for them if I could learn to do this without all the knots."

The raven's eyes narrowed and he cocked his head. "It just takes practice, my boy. Here, try this." And with that, he began to show Westly how to weave the threads together without tangling them.

They worked at it late into the night. When Westly finally got back to Log Hallow, the fires had all died down, and everyone lay wrapped up in sleep, even Zug Zug, who snored happily in his hammock bed. Tired but happy, Westly found his spot. He curled up and fell asleep and dreamed of big, beautiful perfect webs.

Over the next few weeks, Westly worked alongside his insect friends during the day. At night he would visit the raven, who would show him how to weave different patterns. It wasn't long before the small clearing outside the keyhole had dozens of webs stretched between tree branches and tall stalks of grass. Some were better than others, but all were beautiful.

One clear cold morning, as the insects got ready for another day, the dragonfly gave everyone a surprise.

"Because of Westly's webs, we're two whole days ahead of schedule. Everyone take a break and we'll meet back here after lunch."

A loud cheer rang through the clearing and everyone hurried over to Westly to thank him.

It took Westly a moment to extract himself from his happy friends, and even more time to lose Zug Zug, who followed him everywhere now. But when the ants began a game of kickball, the small fly happily joined in. Westly crept away.

"Oh Mr. Raven? Mr. Raaaven?" Westly called as he wiggled through the keyhole. "Where are you?"

The raven hopped down from where he'd been perched at the very top of a young sapling, the jewels and baubles on his coat winking in the sunshine. He dropped another bowl onto the growing pile.

"Well, hello, my young friend. This is an unexpected surprise. What brings you out of the menagerie at this time of the morning?" All of the webs were covered in dewdrops and glistened as if they had been made of diamonds. The raven was careful to not become entangled in them.

Westly beamed happily at his friend, no longer afraid of his long pointed beak or his beady red eyes.

"It's terrific," exclaimed Westly. "You wouldn't believe how far I've come. I used my web to carry raspberries yesterday! And today the dragonfly gave us the morning off because we're so caught up with our tasks. Everyone was singing and dancing—the centipede doesn't even grumble at me anymore!"

As excited words tumbled out of Westly's mouth, the raven sat and listened, a tiny smile at the corner of his mouth.

"And, and, oh, it was just amazing," Westly said, letting out a sigh of joy.

The raven smiled widely. "I really admire you, Westly. Not just for yesterday's adventure—and that was indeed a remarkable story—but because you are a true student. You've listened, you've learned, you've grown. And all in such a short time. In fact, you've learned almost all I have to teach you."

Westly beamed under the praise.

But the Raven's smile slowly faded.

"Mr. Raven?" Westly asked. He watched as the raven pulled a beautiful glass box from inside his fancy robe. He pulled a couple of jeweled rings from the box and slid them onto his feathers.

Though he couldn't make out exactly what they were, Westly could see them sparkle in the sunlight, not unlike the other trinkets and baubles the raven wore. "Your rings are beautiful," Westly commented.

"Oh, these old things," the raven said, fluttering his feathers so again Westly was unable to get a closer look. "They're a reminder of days long past, my little friend. Really, Westly, more than anything, I want to tell you how grateful I am that you came to me today to share in your joy. It means so much."

Shaking his head, Westly replied, "You're my friend. That's what friends do."

"Thank you, Westly," the raven repeated. Then he sighed and wiped his feathered hands across his eyes. "Winter is coming, and I'm afraid I must fly away today."

The raven's words shook Westly to the core. "Wait—what? Fly away? No!"

"Yes, I'm afraid I must. Haven't you noticed the days are growing shorter and the nights colder? If I stay I'm afraid I'll freeze to death out here."

The thought of not being able to see his friend every day sat like a stone in the pit of Westly's stomach but he *had* noticed the change in the weather now that he was standing out in the open air. "But surely you'll come back once winter is over?" Westly asked.

"No, I'm afraid not," the raven said, his head sagging. "It's such a great distance between here and the sunny spot I fly to in the winter. I'm not sure my old bones could make the journey back again."

"But—but that's terrible!" Westly exclaimed, hopping to the ground. He could feel the tears welling up in his eyes. "I don't know what I'll do without you."

"Here now, I didn't want to upset you." He took hold of Westly's tiny hands. "Not today, of all days. Let's not talk of such sad news here in our last few moments together. Let's make this memory a happy one." The raven smiled widely down at Westly. "Now, in my country we exchange gifts at the parting of ways. It's a way we can remember each other and our friendship. And that's why I've shared with you all of my knowledge of spiders. It's been my gift to you all along."

Westly's heart sank. "Mr. Raven, I would have brought you something, if only you had told me."

The raven smiled down at Westly. "You needn't worry, my little friend. You have my gift to you. That should be enough."

"Oh no, Mr. Raven, you've given me so much. And I'd do anything for a friend in return. Please tell me! What can I give that will remind you of me?"

"Really, Westly, it's not—"

"Please, Mr. Raven." Westly's big eyes began to fill again.

"Of course, dear friend. If you insist." The raven smiled and his red eyes narrowed.

Westly thought for a moment. "Could I make you

something out of a web? I could weave some cloth for you and you could add it to your robes."

"Oh, that *is* a good idea, but . . . I don't think something that delicate would survive the trip. What about something more permanent? Something that sparkles?"

"Of course!" exclaimed Westly. "I could get you one of the crystals from the chandelier."

"That's a lovely thought. But I have so many like those already," the raven murmured, pointing to the glittering gems on his chest. He tapped his chin. "Say, I know. I've seen it through the glass. A small gold key, hidden behind the vines. It would be the perfect addition to my collection."

"A key?" Westly tried to remember if he'd seen a key in the menagerie before.

"I saw it when I first arrived on the island. But of course, it's out of my reach. It is so shiny and beautiful."

Westly beamed. "I'd be happy to get it for you, Mr. Raven."

"You are a true friend, Westly," exclaimed the raven. "It might be rather dangerous, though. You see, it hangs on the wall near a dark and rotting well. Are you sure you want to risk it?"

Westly hesitated. The well's darkness had always scared him. Rumor had it that whispers could be heard coming from the darkness, whispers that could draw a careless caterpillar into its depths. Once, as a young caterpillar, he'd almost fallen in but had been saved by his father. The thought of going back sent chills down all eight legs. However, if it meant getting the key for his friend, then he would do it. He had to.

"I'm not afraid of the well," Westly said, his voice shaking a bit.

The raven smiled. "Then look for it on the wall, between the windowpanes. A shiny key on a tiny nail. I'm sure it is worthless to those in the menagerie, just a forgotten relic. But to me, it would be priceless. A way to remember my little spider friend, Westly."

Westly beamed. "I'll find it. I promise."

"Splendid! What a friend you are. Do be careful though. And make sure to keep all those tricks I taught you handy. You'll likely need them."

Westly nodded and waved as he eagerly crawled back through the keyhole.

Chapter 13

When Westly arrived at the courtyard in the center of the menagerie, he was in such a hurry that he did not realize at first how close he was to his old home. Fluttering wings drew his gaze upward, where he saw a pair of butterflies drifting lazily from one nectar bud to the next, sipping and laughing in quiet conversation. He wondered if he knew them. If he hadn't come out of his cocoon a spider, he would be with them right now. That thought made him pause and watch.

What are they talking about? he wondered. Adult butterflies had always talked about gossip, fashion, dreams, and the like. He thought that his own name would probably arise from time to time, but he imagined it would be in hushed tones—the story of the demon prince. He shuddered.

Though Westly felt a strong urge to get closer, he turned away instead. They would never welcome him back, and certainly not as their Monarch. If his father hadn't been successful at persuading the council to let him stay, no one could have been. Deep in his heart he loved his father for trying.

Shaking sad thoughts from his mind, Westly carefully skirted around the well and began to climb the tangled vines that rose up the side of the menagerie. It took him a little while and a few wrong turns before he saw it. Hanging on a tiny nail halfway up the wall, the shiny key was hidden from sight among thick leaves. Only someone from the outside could have spotted it. Westly smiled. This would be easy.

The leaf on which he sat wobbled a bit before he found the perfect balance. Spooling out a length of silk, he carefully wrapped it around the bottom of the key and began to pull it tight. Except in his excitement, he forgot to check the knot. So when he pulled the key from the nail and it swung out through the leaves, the knot broke and the key went sailing through the air. Westly's heart sank as he watched it disappear down the well's black mouth.

Westly swallowed. He'd been warned to never go near the well. Those who did never returned.

Maybe he could find the raven something else. Another key, perhaps? But he had no idea where he'd find one, and he had no idea what else he could give. No, this was what the raven had asked for. It was what he would remember Westly by. Westly would have to go down into the well to retrieve it.

Lifting his chin and taking a deep breath, he climbed down the vines, crossed the withered grass, and scaled the pock-marked outer wall of the well.

A bad smell hung in the air above the well. Westly wrinkled his nose and peered into the gloomy depths. Bricks held together with rotting wood were covered in moss and gooey sludge. Roots from nearby trees and bushes snaked down the walls and into the inky darkness below, making it hard to see any kind of clear path. If it hadn't been for the faint sound of water dripping, Westly might have thought the well was truly bottomless as his father had always said. The Monarch's constant warnings of the dangers of the well now made perfect sense. It was clearly more dangerous than anything Westly had ever encountered in his lifetime. A butterfly with its wobbling wings would no doubt get stuck; a crawling insect could not

make it down the slimy sides; even most of the flying gardeners, such as the dragonfly, would risk getting snared.

And then there was the darkness below, where the sunlight's fingers could not reach—no creature would be able to
see.

Westly's task felt too hard. He took a step back from the
edge of the well and took a deep breath. Perhaps being a spider
with newly learned tricks would give him an advantage, but
Westly still felt an urge to turn back. He thought again about
finding something else for the raven, but Westly felt obligated
to fulfill the deepest desire of the raven's heart. He had to get
the key.

Westly stepped up to the edge and peered down. He
chewed on his lip for a moment, then an idea popped into
his head. Just below the lip of the well a jagged piece of wood
had broken away from the wall. If he attached a thread to the
wood, he could lower himself into the well and never have to
touch the walls.

Pleased with his idea, Westly pulled out a length of thread
and began weaving the intricate knots that the raven had
taught him—this time making sure that they were all tight and
secure.

When all was ready, Westly held his breath and swung out

over the deep blackness of the well. With a pounding heart, he began to descend.

As he traveled down, Westly's eyes adjusted to the dim light, making it easier to see just a little way ahead. The smell Westly had noticed earlier grew stronger and he had to plug his nose. More than once, Westly ran into places where rotten wood blocked his way. He had to slip across the gooey edges and continue onward. Each time he touched the wood, the well gave an audible groan as though it was about to collapse. But the old structure held and Westly was able to continue on.

Eventually the light disappeared altogether, and Westly found himself entirely alone. He lowered himself more slowly so he wouldn't crash into any unseen obstacles. He thought he heard a faint moaning coming from somewhere above him and a shiver raced up his spine, but in the darkness he could see nothing. So when his feet touched something cold and wet, the shock made him yell. His thread unspooled and he dropped into a thick slimy pool.

Westly had found the bottom of the well.

As he sputtered and splashed about, he smacked into something hard just below the surface. He clutched at it in a desperate effort to keep from sinking, but it seemed to be stuck in the mud.

Shivering in the dark, only his nose above the surface of

the pool, Westly ran his free hands around the object. It was the key! Relieved, he began pulling it to the surface.

He was so focused on the key that when something in the pool oozed around his back, it made him jump. He twisted his head around, trying to see, but the darkness was too thick. A shiver ran up his spine and he knew instantly that he was in danger.

Westly began to pull more urgently at the key. Each tug was agonizingly painful. For a brief moment he had to pull with his head completely under the water to try to get the key out of the mud. He sputtered when he finally surfaced.

He heard the moaning again. Then, with a sickening feeling in his stomach, Westly realized that it wasn't actually coming from above. It was coming from all around him.

He pulled once more with all his strength, and at last the key broke out of the muck. The water suddenly began churning; the moaning grew louder and louder until, like the sucking of an inward breath, whatever was moving around him gasped.

"Ahhh—someone is here. It's fallen into our well. We can smell it, can't we?" Westly nearly screamed. He clutched the shiny key tightly as he realized that the moaning had been the combined voices of dozens—hundreds?—of creatures lurking in the darkness of the well.

Westly fought against the panic that was rising inside him, but as he scrabbled up his thread, a slurping noise echoed around him as whatever it was slid up and around the walls, surrounding him from above and below.

"What is it? What has fallen into our well?" the voices asked.

His legs trembling, Westly clung to his web, his feet clutching the key.

"Yessss, it smells so good."

To calm down, Westly bit his tongue and inhaled slowly through his nose. There was no running away from these creatures, even if Westly tried. They had him surrounded—whatever they were.

"M-m-my name's Westly," he called into the dark. "Who—who are you?"

"Ahhh—a spider. We haven't had one of your kind join us in ages," the voices said, sounding gleeful.

Westly tried not to think what those words meant. "How did you know what I am? Can you see me?"

"We are worms," the voices said. "We don't see. We smell—everything."

"Oh. Okay. Well, that's interesting. So, um," Westly gulped, "I'm just passing through. I dropped something, you see—I mean, you smell. Wait. Not 'you smell' like, you know,

you smell, but . . . Never mind. I have what I came for now. I'll be going—"

"Going? You just arrived. Come to us," the voices hissed with a laugh.

"Oh. Um, no thank you," said Westly. "I appreciate the offer, but there's someone waiting for me." All eight of his legs were trembling. "A-a friend who's leaving soon. I must hurry."

The worms laughed. "But we're hungry for company, too."

Suddenly, the unified voice of the worms broke into a dozen smaller voices, each with a different pitch and all talking over each other.

"It smells so good!"

"Let's eat it now!"

"Pull it down! Pull it down!"

The voices broke off as a million malicious giggles echoed around the chamber. A wall of slime seemed to close in on him.

Westly was more scared than he'd ever been. He didn't stop to think, he just acted. Pulling hard on his thread, Westly began to climb, ignoring the slimy bodies as he shot upwards.

The worms swirled around him, and as he climbed towards the sunlight he could see them now: a mass of pale tubes slithering around the sides of the chamber, withered, wrinkled, and twisted against each other like wet tree roots. They crawled blindly through the labyrinth of vines in a wild search for him.

"Where are you going, little spider? Stay here in the well with us." Their voices hissed and hummed around him.

"It's warm down here. You'll be warm and safe with us."

Westly climbed harder. The key felt heavier and heavier.

"It's better than going back. You won't have to think

anymore. You won't have to be afraid. You belong here. Safe. Warm. Come to us, come," the worms crooned. "Come . . ."

With each whisper, Westly's eyes drooped and the key grew heavier.

"No one who comes down the well ever leaves. Come, stay with us. You're welcome here. You're welcome."

"No. I can't." Westly was so tired he could barely move his arms. Maybe it *would* be easier to let go and sleep. One thought kept him going. "I need to get the key to the raven," Westly repeated. "I need to get the . . ."

As Westly climbed into the dim light he lost the strength to keep his eyes open. "You don't need the key. It belongs to a life of pain. All you need is us." There was some desperation in the voices now, but Westly did not understand why.

"It's not for me," he whispered. "It's a gift—"

"A gift?"

"—for my friend . . ." With one last mighty heave, Westly pulled himself into the warm sunlight and his eyes popped open.

"It can't!" the worms screamed.

"No one ever leaves!"

"It has to stay with us!"

"Eat it! Eat it!"

Westly threw the key over the side of the well, then

scrambled up and over himself. Below him the well groaned as if all the rotting wood was about to collapse. Looking back to see if any worms had followed him, Westly saw them clearly. Ghostly pale, long, round slimy bodies twisted and writhed around each other as they tried to reach him, their mouths black gaping holes. But they seemed unwilling to enter the sunlight. Westly shuddered and dropped into the grass next to the key.

Chapter 14

After Westly had caught his breath and his little legs had stopped shaking, he sat up and examined the key. It seemed to be undamaged. Beneath the spatters of mud and slime, it sparkled just as bright as it had when it was hanging on the wall. Westly smiled and began dragging it back through the forest.

It took several hours to get it through the thick undergrowth, but when Westly finally reached the brush that marked the hidden door, he felt tired but happy. He was going to be able to repay the raven for his kindnesses.

A sense of pride filled the little spider and he could not wait to see the look on the raven's face. Then he looked up at the keyhole and realized that there was no way he was going to be able to get the key all the way through that small space.

Westly's forehead wrinkled. All his pride fizzled out. He'd come this far only to fail. Westly dropped the key and put his head in his hands. A small tear leaked from his eyes. But then he noticed that there was a space beneath the door. A narrow strip just big enough to fit . . .

Westly jumped up and dragged the key over to the narrow gap. Pushing it in front of him, he held his breath. The key slid through easily.

"Yes!" Westly exclaimed happily. Then he wiggled through after it.

Beyond the ocean, the sun had just set, leaving the horizon a deep orange. The air had begun to cool for the night. As Westly began to pull the key into the clearing he noticed that some of his webs had disappeared, but he was too happy to wonder about it beyond noticing.

"Mr. Raven?" Westly called. The clearing remained empty and silent. "Mr. Raven!" Westly called more loudly. "Are you here?"

A shadow glided down from the trees, followed by a familiar flutter of wings.

Westly smiled. "Oh, Mr. Raven! I'm sorry I took so long. I was so worried you'd leave without saying goodbye. And you're not going to believe what I have."

"Oh, it is so good to see you! I've been quite anxious, you know. Goodness! What happened to you?"

Westly realized that he was still muddy from the well. He smiled sheepishly. "I dropped the key into the well. But I

climbed down and got it," he added, unable to hide the pride in his voice. Westly proudly held it up for his friend to see.

The raven smiled and his red eyes narrowed. He stretched out his fingers and stroked the key softly. "I did it," he whispered.

Westly's smile faltered. Had he heard correctly? No. No it must have been a mistake. Westly stepped back as the raven reached down and gently lifted up the key.

"Years and years of searching. I feared I might never see the day. Oh! And now . . . they're mine. They're all mine!" the raven said, clutching the key to his chest.

"Do you want to hear the story of how I . . ." Westly began, but then changed his mind when it appeared the raven wasn't listening to him. "I—I guess it doesn't matter. I'm just happy you like it."

The raven did not appear to even hear him.

As the raven continued to ignore him, Westly's joy turned into confusion. A few of the hairs on the back of his neck pricked up too, and he glanced around nervously.

"Is everything all right, Mr. Raven?"

Letting out a great sigh, the tall bird's eyes landed on Westly. He answered, "Oh dear, oh dear. What a tremendous reward for so long a journey. Westly, I knew you could do it. Such talent in such a tiny body. Just think—if you hadn't been born a spider you wouldn't have accomplished such a dangerous task. But you did, and so well. It's too bad, really. I've enjoyed teaching you. I really have, but I can't risk having you run and tell any of your little insect friends about me, especially the butterflies. I've waited too long for this, Westly. You've got to understand. It's nothing personal." The raven lifted up one of his large, clawed feet.

Westly's eyes widened. His instinct warned him to run, but he couldn't. He stood rooted to the spot. "M-m-mister Raven? What are you doing?"

"It's your last lesson, Westly," the raven growled. "If you truly want to understand what it is to be a spider, then," he stomped his foot, smashing Westly between it and the soft dirt, "you need to die like one."

The clearing fell silent as the raven pulled his foot away. Westly's crumpled body lay between the blades of grass, his eyes closed. From behind one of the bushes, the raven pulled out two sticks between which hung one of the Westly's strongest webs. A net.

The raven smiled. He set the net aside and reached for the key. Sliding it into the keyhole, he paused before he turned it. "Yes, yes! I've waited so long for this! Soon the butterflies will be mine!"

He turned the key and heard a click. The raven pushed the door—it cracked open an inch, then stopped. He pushed again but the old door refused to move. The raven looked through the glass and saw the tangled vines clinging to it, holding it shut. Anger surged through him. He'd waited too long to be held back by some plants. With a growl, he slammed against the door. The wood creaked in protest and the glass shuddered. Once more and the wood frame splintered and glass exploded everywhere.

The menagerie was open. The raven grabbed his net and flew inside.

Chapter 15

It was dark when Westly awoke. For a moment he thought he must have had a nightmare but when he tried to move and his entire body protested he knew it hadn't been a dream. The raven—his best friend—had tried to kill him.

But why?

Westly rolled over and tried to stand, but his wobbly legs wouldn't hold him—at least not yet—so he looked around instead. What he saw broke his heart. The key he'd risked his life to get sat in the keyhole, the door broken open. He heard screaming from inside the menagerie.

Forcing his legs to work, he scrambled back into the menagerie and up onto the window where he could see everything. With horror he watched as the raven swooped around the chandelier, filling his net with butterflies. Some ran, some tried to hide, others tried to herd the caterpillars to safety. But none of them got away.

Westly sank down on the windowsill and buried his head

in his hands. *He* had done this. He had made the web that the raven now used as a net. He had brought the key that the raven had used to open the old door. He had known in his heart that the raven was bad, but it didn't matter. The raven had showed him kindness when no one else had. The raven had tricked him.

Westly began to cry.

A quarter of an hour passed; Westly watched from the distance as the impossibly large bird finished destroying Westly's former home and snatching the last few members of his butterfly family out of the air. And when the great beast had finished, he began arranging branches and twigs around the spokes of the chandelier. The raven was building a nest.

Suddenly, there was a loud buzzing sound and something crashed into Westly's head. He leapt up and opened his mouth to scream, but a hand clamped over it and pulled him back down.

"Shh!" his captor hissed. "Don't draw its attention."

The thing that had run into Westly's head moved around to his shoulder, buzzed in his ear, and gave him an affectionate nuzzle. Westly breathed a sigh of relief as he realized it was Zug Zug and the dragonfly.

The dragonfly pointed to the foot of the door, and Westly

saw the other menagerie bugs quietly making their way through the vines to the outside.

"Zug Zug, off you go now. Out where it's safe," the dragonfly said, waving him away. But the little fly refused, dodging the dragonfly's arms.

"Okay, fine, you can stay—but be quiet. Listen, Westly, we don't know how this happened—we didn't even know it could. But we've got to get out of here. The winged monster has taken all the butterflies. It's dangerous, and, well . . ."

Westly's eyes went wide as he waited.

". . . it's just a matter of time before it comes after us."

Westly moaned softly.

"We were just sitting around the fire, wondering where you were, when that monster showed up and, as you see . . ." the dragonfly said. "I'm glad we found you. We were afraid it had gotten you too."

They watched in silence for a moment as the raven pulled out his glass display box, now filled with butterflies. With a shout of glee, the raven began to dance around.

"All this time," Westly whispered, "He was just waiting. Waiting to come inside and destroy us."

"I suppose he might have been," the dragonfly answered. "But there's no way to know for sure. And there's no time either way. We have to go—now."

"But what about the butterflies?" asked Westly. "We can't leave them."

"I'm afraid there's nothing we can do. You've seen that creature—he'll do the same to us. We have to get out while we can."

It was too much to comprehend. The idea that the raven had been using him all along, planning only to crush him and do . . . do who knows what with the butterflies—it felt like getting smashed by the raven all over again.

"Where are we going?" Westly asked.

"Haven't figured that out yet. We don't know what's out there, so we'll just have to wing it. Listen, Westly. I mean it. We have to go—now."

Westly nodded, but still stood frozen. Zug Zug buzzed anxiously next to him. The dragonfly grabbed Westly and pulled him down from the window.

As Westly fell quietly in line with the other insects, his mind churned. How was he supposed to know that the raven would do this? The raven had acted as harmless as a regular insect—until now. And why weren't the butterflies more prepared? Didn't they know that this was bound to happen someday? Shouldn't they have had a plan?

As he thought about it, he realized that he had known this might happen. He was aware that his ancestors had locked them in the menagerie for a reason: for protection. Westly also knew that he should not have trusted the raven when he first met him, but he had pushed those feelings away.

Now, less than a hundred yards behind him, his family and all his friends were paying the price. He had no idea what the raven intended to do with them, but Westly suspected that they would never, ever see the light of day again.

Thinking about the loss of all that good cheer, music, and sunny afternoons among the butterflies was too much. He didn't even want to be with the other bugs; it was his fault they were marching away from their home. Tears began to pour down his face. Quietly, he moved to the side of the line, slumped in the grass, and curled into a ball. Zug Zug buzzed around his head, but Westly ignored him.

A soft sound of footprints on the ground grew nearer, and then a kind, familiar voice said, "Come on now, Westly. You're falling behind."

Westly didn't look up. He had no need. He knew it was the moth.

"Things are not always as they seem. There are dozens of adventures awaiting us. You need to get up and meet them. Things will work out, I promise. You'll see."

Westly did not answer.

The warm and fuzzy creature sat down beside him. "I

know how you feel, you know—having life suddenly turn in a direction you did not expect."

"You have no idea," Westly whispered.

"Oh, don't I? Do you think you're the only one who has had to make hard choices? Do you think you're the only one who has had to struggle to discover who they truly are?"

Westly thought about it for a moment, then shook his head. "That's not what I meant," he mumbled into his arms.

"Then what *did* you mean?" the moth asked gently.

"I just meant that . . . you'd be better off without me. All of you would."

"Is that so? And why's that, Westly? You're one of the most talented creatures I've ever had the honor of meeting. Why would you think that anyone would be better off without you?" Westly could not tell the moth about the guilt he felt, and so he only swallowed a sob. The moth nodded. "Well, let's just say this night has been hard for everyone. But if we're going to get through it, we must get through it together."

Westly nodded and whispered, "Okay."

"That's it. Now, listen to me. Things always look darkest before the dawn. Things will turn out all right in the end. They always do. But you're going to need to get up first."

"I can't," answered Westly, wiping a tear off his nose.

"I thought we'd been through this—"

"I mean I've got to go back," he said, standing up and shaking out his arms. Zug Zug buzzed happily around his head.

"To the menagerie?"

"The butterflies—they're my family."

The moth didn't say anything for minute. Then, "That's very brave of you, but . . ."

Westly was no longer listening. He took a step towards the menagerie, but then stopped again. "Actually, you're right. I think I have to go find everyone else first. How far ahead are they?"

"About ten yards, I'd guess. Are you all right? Westly, wait up. I'm coming too."

With the moth and Zug Zug fluttering behind him, Westly bolted in the direction the others had gone. The words the moth had said to Westly sank deeply into his soul. The only way things could turn out all right would be to go back. But before he could do that, he would need help.

Chapter 16

Together Westly, the moth, and Zug Zug sped along, following the other insects' tracks that led alongside a black river. The path led them through the woods and over a field of barren rock until they came to the beach, where they found the insects still marching.

"Stop, everyone," Westly cried. "You've got to stop!"

When Westly reached the front, he waved the dragonfly down. "We've got to turn back—we can't just leave the butterflies like that. They need to be rescued."

As everyone halted, the dragonfly settled in the sand next to Westly. "Why?" he asked.

"Because they'll die if we don't do anything."

"But if we return, a lot more of us will die, too."

"And that might happen out here just as easily," Westly said, pointing further down the beach where churning waves rolled up and down.

"True, but in one direction the danger is certain, not so the other," the dragonfly said, and he waved for the others to keep moving.

"Why should we care anyway, Wes?" a voice shouted from the back of the line. It was the centipede, and he gave Westly a grumpy glare as he passed. "All they've ever done is bat their pretty wings at you and me. And by the looks of it, that big feathery beast wants 'em for the same reason. Now don't you go tellin' us they aren't gettin' what they deserve."

"But," Westly protested, "how can we live knowing that we just left them? We'd have no honor."

"There's no honor in suicide," the centipede growled.

Biting his lip, Westly pleaded one last time. "Mr. Dragonfly, please listen. I have a plan." The dragonfly gave Westly one of his penetrating stares. Westly stared back at him.

Finally, with a heavy breath, the dragonfly held up his arms to signal all to stop. "Very well then, little Westly. Let's hear your plan."

The spider took a deep breath and began to pace in front of them. "It's true that the butterflies look down on us. I know it as well as anyone here. And it's true that they're lazy and unappreciative. But we've been known to be that as well. So I can understand why no one here feels an obligation to return. But though they may not be the best neighbors, they're a part of the menagerie, the place we've called home since the day we were born. We've put our hearts into that glass world. We've pruned, we've harvested—we've watched it grow. There's not much in there that hasn't been affected by us, one way or another. So we've had differences with the butterflies—so what? Aren't differences a part of life? Just look at me and the trouble I caused. But you stuck with me, even though I was different and clumsy. And now our friendship grows every day."

Westly took a deep breath. "So why couldn't it be the same with the butterflies? We don't always have control over what happens to us, but we do have control over how we choose to react. We have control over who we choose to be. All of us are family, whether we live at the top or the bottom of the menagerie. We need each other. We rely on each other. And we can choose to grow. Back at our home is the biggest opportunity we've had in a lifetime, and we'll never get another one like it again. We have an opportunity to save our home, our family. If we leave, we're dead inside already. So who's with me? Who will fight for our home and our family?"

For a long while the only answer was silence. Sweat began to drip down Westly's face. He wasn't sure he'd even convinced himself.

Then the centipede declared, "You know, the boy's right. I'm with ya, Wes." And then he mumbled quietly, "I ain't gonna let that kid have a tougher shell than me."

A murmur started
at the back of the group
and several of the insects began nodding to each other.
The dragonfly stepped
forward. He looked
sternly into the faces
of all his clan, then turned
to Westly and said, "We're in."

Chapter 17

Wreathed in moon-light and the chilly night air, the insects made their way back through the orchard to the splintered door of the menagerie. Westly really had no idea what they were going to do to defeat the raven—he just knew they had to. He'd been amazed at the passion of the words that had come out of his mouth. Though he'd made it up on the spot, he felt the truth behind what he had said. They *were* a family. All of them. Pollinators and gardeners alike. In order to save themselves they needed to save the butterflies, but he wasn't quite sure how to do that.

A feeling of guilt pushed its way to the surface. Should he tell them about his friendship with the raven? About the key? Westly shook his head. No. No, right now they needed to figure out how to get rid of the raven. His blame could come later. He pushed the guilt back down. If they defeated the raven maybe it wouldn't matter.

Once inside the menagerie they climbed the walls and the vines until they had a good view of the chandelier.

The raven had nearly finished a nest of twigs, leaves, and mud in the very center of the chandelier. Surrounding the edges of the nest they could see dozens of glass collecting boxes, each full of panicked butterflies. In the center of his nest, the raven had built a small fire with a metal pot hanging over it, its contents steaming and boiling. As the raven stirred the pot, he sang:

Sweet little crispies, laid out in a row:
One at the head and one at the toe.
Put them in a necklace; make a lovely jew'l;
O how they'll smile all eternity for you.
Set 'em while they're hot and wear 'em when they're cold.
What a lovely potion to keep from growing old!

He sang the tune over and over, and then put the spoon

aside and stretched out, his back against one of the glass boxes as if to take a nap.

The insects turned to each other, puzzled. Westly was still bewildered about what was happening, but he didn't want to wait any longer. So he waved for everyone to follow him back to the ground.

On the ground, the dragonfly gathered every-one together in a circle. "What was that horrible song?" someone from the back asked. "I think he's going to eat them," someone else said, hor-rified.

"We're going to have to do this right away," Westly said. "While he sleeps. We'll only get one chance."

"I say we hit 'im on the head with a rock," the grumpy centipede suggested.

The beetles nodded, but the others shifted their eyes to the ground.

The praying mantis shook his head. "I don't know. That would have to be a pretty big rock. There has to be a better way."

Westly nodded.

Always the peacemaker, the dragon-fly spoke up. "Maybe we could just talk to him. We could tell him about how the butterflies are our neighbors and we—"

"No, it won't do any good," Westly interrupted. "He—you saw how he's treating those butterflies. Insects to him are just objects to be toyed with. We couldn't trust whatever he'd say."

"Wes is right," a beetle added. "We've all heard since we were kids that creatures on the outside aren't to be trusted."

Another wave of guilt hit Westly but he stomped it back. "Let's think. We've got to do this our way. We've got to think of him like a weed. Right? He's a weed that's growing in our garden. What do we do with weeds?"

"We tear 'em out by the root," several said at once.

"A plant has roots so it can always draw water and nutrients from the soil," Westly mused. "But . . . he always has to draw breath from the air. That's it! That's his weakness!"

"I like it," the dragonfly agreed. "If we cut off his air, maybe we can weaken him enough to tie him up and carry him out of the menagerie."

"We've got to do it by surprise," the mantis added. "No warning, or it'll turn into a battle, and the odds are against us."

"Agreed," Westly said. "We'll use my webs to wrap him and carry him out the door."

"And that will be the end of him," a beetle growled.

Everyone nodded. With grim faces, heavy steps, and

clenched hands, the insects carefully made their way through the menagerie. The crawling insects climbed to the ceiling, the flyers soared to the trees, and all waited while Westly crawled to a spot directly above the raven. He looked down at the beast he'd thought was his friend and realized again that he'd ignored his most basic instincts. Westly had felt from the beginning that the raven was dangerous, but he'd been desperate for someone, anyone, to notice him. But he'd pushed those feelings away, and this was the result. Whatever else happened, Westly had to make this right.

Taking a deep breath, Westly put his hand high in the air and threw it down with a shout: "For home, for family, for freedom—*charge!*"

As if from nowhere insects began dropping from the sky like rain. The raven woke with a start to find dozens of ants, beetles, centipedes, and other insects crawling over his jeweled cloak, headed for his throat.

For a moment he froze. Then like a snake shedding its skin, the raven slid out of his cloak and quickly flipped it inside out, trapping the insects inside. He tied knots at both ends and picked up his now-full bag of bugs.

"Well, well, well," the raven said happily, "what a pleasant surprise."

Chapter 18

When the insects found themselves trapped, their fierce determination quickly changed to panic. They pleaded to be let go and struggled to find a way out.

They heard the raven talking to himself softly. "I'm not really sure if I'll have enough resin to go around. I suppose I could always make another batch if I have to . . ."

Suddenly the knot at one end was untied, letting in the dim blue light of the moon. Like bees diving into nectar, they all scrambled for the opening only to find that it led straight into a glass collection box already half full of butterflies.

The space was so small they had to squeeze in on top of each other. When they were all in, the raven snapped the lid shut and shook it to get them all to settle. One great eye fixed on the box, the raven bent down to examine each more closely.

"Some wonderful species! The beetles will make beautiful brooches, and I do believe I see a praying mantis—I've always wanted one of those. The rest of you . . . I might be able to find a use for you . . . maybe."

"Please don't eat us," one of the butterflies said, her voice quivering with fear.

The raven threw back his head and laughed. "Dear little insect, of course I'm not going to *eat* you. That would be such a waste of beauty." He reached around the box and pointed at the metal pot sitting above the fire. "I apologize. Here, let me show you what I have in store for you."

Angling the box around so that the insects could see more clearly, he moved over to the fire. "You've actually got quite a treat coming your way. That's right. You see, most creatures simply disappear into the earth forever—forgotten almost immediately. You little beauties deserve a much better place in history. And for that I've created a more noble, fitting method by which you may be remembered."

The raven gestured at his robes. "Have you noticed my jewelry? It's lovely, isn't it? Really, there's nothing quite like it on all the islands. I would know because I make it myself. Allow me to show you how I create these exquisite jewels. It's more complicated than it looks, believe it or not. But see here . . ." the raven said. He captured a little of the boiling liquid with a wooden spoon and poured it into a shallow bowl. He swished

the liquid around for a while and then tilted
the bowl forward so the insects could see.

"This is my jewelry resin. While it's
warm, it's still a liquid. And this means
that I can . . . Here, let me show you."

He picked a leaf from the angel
ivy and placed it in the bowl. The
clear, sticky goo easily covered the leaf
without affecting its shape.

"See how the leaf sparkles, even here
in the moonlight? It's quite beautiful, don't you think? Well,
once the resin dries, this leaf will look exactly as it does now.
Forever."

The insects stared at him, still not quite understanding
what the raven meant.

"Just think of it—forever! Creatures for generations will
see it in all its natural beauty . . ."

Crammed into a corner of the collecting box, Westly had
a clear view of the raven and his strange experiment. Keeping
himself scrunched into a ball, he hoped he could remain unno-
ticed. But as he listened to the raven's explanation and looked
at the jewelry on his robes, the blood drained out of Weslty's
face. It dawned on him what the terrible beast was doing.

Somewhere in another area of the box the dragonfly made the connection also.

"This is a fate worse than death!" the dragonfly said.

"Oh, now don't say that," the raven said. He pulled a pair of earrings from out of a pocket and put them on. "I fly all over the world, visiting exotic places. Each gets to add to my glorious outfit. And soon you'll be part of that wonderful display!" As he turned, the insects could see that the earrings were made of perfectly preserved honeybees.

The panic the insects had felt earlier faded in comparison with what now exploded out of them. They shouted, pounded, and even knocked themselves against the glass. Some fell to the bottom of the box, too exhausted and scared to move.

"There, there, now," the raven said, patting the box as he put it back in place. "I'm sure it doesn't hurt very much."

And with that the raven turned back to the boiling brew.

Westly felt panic swell within him. It was one thing to be betrayed and stepped on. It was quite another to be turned into a brooch. He couldn't imagine a worse fate.

Then he looked over his shoulder and saw his father, the Monarch, crowded into a corner of the box and his panic grew. Oh yes, there *was* a fate worse than becoming one of the raven's jewels—facing his father.

Fearing that if his father saw him he'd reveal who Westly

really was, he crept into the tangle of bodies and prayed that he would not be noticed by either his father or the raven.

The panic and chaos continued until one butterfly with a delicate frame and beautiful large pink wings wiggled into the center of the commotion, held out her arms, and shouted, "All right, all right! Everybody calm down." Westly recognized her immediately. It was Sara, his childhood friend. The dragonfly saw her too and called for the gardeners to calm themselves. It took a minute or two for the fluttering to finally die down.

Sara spoke. "We need to stay calm, everyone. Everything's going to be all right. It's not over yet— we'll find a way out."

"The little lady is right," said the dragonfly.

He locked eyes with her and she met his gaze respectfully.

The dragonfly continued, looking a little abashed. "We meant to help, but clearly we only made things worse."

"What do you mean you meant to help?" The Monarch pushed

through the crowd until he stood before the dragonfly. "Why would you help us?"

Westly, who had crept forward to get a closer look at his friend, moved back into the crowd.

"We helped because we knew you were in trouble," replied the dragonfly. "But our plan didn't work."

Tension filled the air as the butterflies realized that these creatures whom they so often ignored had tried to save their lives.

"Bless you . . ." Sara whispered.

And with that the tension disappeared. A murmur of surprise passed among the butterflies, and then came soft words of thanks.

"I suppose, I suppose . . . honestly—" the Monarch began, his chest swelling and his face full of emotion.

"What he means to say," Sara said, "is that we all owe you our thanks."

"No," the dragonfly replied, shaking his head. He looked around at his own clan, who all looked back with level gazes and calm smiles. "We all live together in this menagerie."

"It's an act of pure nobility, and of the finest order," the Monarch said. He put his hand out to the dragonfly, who paused and took it slowly. Their handshake gradually grew more confident until finally they were smiling openly at each other, and the Monarch laughed. He began moving around the others to shake hands, chuckling and hugging every creature he could reach. Westly tried to keep his distance, though his father's words and actions surprised him. If his father could change his mind about the gardeners, could he change his mind about Westly? The little spider watched his father make his way through the crowd.

When the Monarch approached the centipede, however, the skinny creature stuck a hand out for only a moment and then pulled it back. He glared at the Monarch and murmured, "Are you sure you want to touch it? I've been eating dirt, you know . . ."

The dragonfly started to protest but the Monarch waved the comment away, shaking his head. "No, he's quite right. Kind of silly, the way we've acted all these years." He puffed out his chest and said, "An apology is in order."

"An apology?" the dragonfly asked.

"We've been the poorest of neighbors, and the only thing worse is that it took getting caught for us to realize how silly we've been acting."

A murmur of agreement rippled through the crowd. In that moment the differences between the butterflies and the gardeners slowly melted away.

"That's all right, Your Highness," replied the dragonfly.

"We haven't been any better. In fact, I really shouldn't be the one taking credit for this. If I'd had my way we'd have been long gone by now. You see, I wanted to run away, but there was one of us who had the courage to come back. Where is Westly, anyhow?"

Westly's heart raced as he frantically looked for a place to hide. He couldn't face his father or the gardeners. Not with all his secrets.

As the dragonfly looked for the little spider, a hushed whisper ran through the butterflies. "Did you say *Westly?*" the Monarch asked.

"Yes, yes. Just a minute, and you'll meet him," said the dragonfly.

Zug Zug was the first to spot Westly and zipped happily around his friend's head. Westly tried to shoo him away, but the many-handed centipede grabbed the little spider from his hiding place, and pushed him into the open. "Here he is. Not much to look at, but just wait till you get to know 'im."

"Westly!" the Monarch shouted as he rushed forward.

And before Westly could say anything, his father wrapped him up in his arms and squeezed and squeezed.

"Oh, my boy! My beautiful boy," the Monarch said. "Where have you been? We've been worried sick about you."

"I, you—you were *worried* about me?" Westly whispered.

"I thought that you wouldn't want me anymore, seeing that I'm . . . not a butterfly."

"Wouldn't want you?" the Monarch exclaimed. "Why, we'd already decided that none of this changed a thing when we noticed you were gone. And we searched for you for so long, but we found no sign of you anywhere." The Monarch wiped tears from his eyes and laughed. "And here you are after all this time. I was so worried I'd never see you again."

"I'm sorry, Father," Westly said, a warm feeling spreading through his body. His father loved him. He always had. Westly had run away for nothing.

The Monarch only turned to the others and called, "Three cheers for Westly! Huzzah! Huzzah! Huzzah!"

As everyone cheered, Westly tried to smile but he knew there were other secrets that still needed to be told. He wanted to tell his father the truth about the raven and what he'd done, but he couldn't bring himself to do it. This was the first moment in his life that his father had shown how much he loved him, and Westly could not bear the thought of spoiling it so quickly—not yet.

Then a familiar voice piped up. "Westly, what is this all about?" The dragonfly was looking very confused.

Westly let go of his father and turned to his friend. "Let me explain. Actually, no, that's going to be really difficult. You see,

I'm a butterfly. I know I don't look like one, but looks aren't everything, right?" He laughed weakly.

He gave everyone a moment to stare at him as though he had gone mad, and then continued, "I was born a caterpillar but I came out of my cocoon a spider. I don't understand it either." He shrugged.

In the back, the blind fuzzy moth smiled. For a moment, everyone forgot about their prison and the raven. But as they tried to make sense of Westly's story, a noise from the nest reminded them where they were.

The Monarch shook his head, still holding Westly's hand, and turned to the dragonfly with a grim look on his face. "Well, we're all in a heap of trouble at the moment. I believe the raven wants to turn us all into jewelry."

All eyes turned to look at the raven, who stood stirring his pots and whistling to himself. "I do believe you're right, Your Highness," the dragonfly replied. "We will all be finished tonight."

"Wait!" Westly said. "You don't seriously believe that, do you?"

"The facts are the facts, my boy. There's not much we can do," the Monarch said.

Putting his hands on his hips, Westly shouted so everyone could hear, "Whoever here is thinking we're going to just lie

down and let that raven turn us into jewels, you can stop right
now. There's no time for that. We need to focus on getting out
of here."

Everyone stared at him blankly.

"Are you with me?" Westly
asked.

The Monarch and the dragonfly
looked at each other, then the dragonfly said, "Tell us your idea, Wes."

Westly smiled. Then, turning to
the butterflies, he pulled out a length
of thread and wove a tiny pattern with
his hands.

"This is called a web. And this is
what it's for . . ."

Chapter 19

A quarter of an hour later, the Monarch knocked heavily—*rap-tap-tap*—on the glass cage.

The first time the raven didn't hear. He was too busy mixing bowls of resin and muttering to himself, "A few dashes more glitter, and a little more blue for this one . . ."

"Your noble ravenness," the Monarch called.

"Hmm?" the raven said, looking up.

The Monarch gave a bow. "Honorable raven, may we request your presence before our humble group?"

"Yes. Yes. In a moment," the raven said absentmindedly. "My resins are almost finished. Then we can have a few final words before we begin."

"Actually, it was about that very thing that we wish to speak to you," the Monarch continued. He cleared his throat. "If I understand correctly, you say you will make jewelry out of us, whether we like it or not?"

"I'm glad you finally understand," the raven answered.

"And there's absolutely nothing we can do to change your mind?"

The raven chuckled. "Of course not. This will be my most beautiful batch ever."

"Very well, then," the Monarch sighed. "In that case, I have something to say on behalf of my creatures. It is a request, and, well . . . I think you might like it."

The raven nodded his head as if he was listening, but he really wasn't. "Forgive my lack of attention, but the resin has to be perfect. Perfect resin for perfect prizes."

"You see, we butterflies have always taken great pride in our appearance. We're very vain creatures. And now, after seeing your beautiful jewels, we realize that we can be preserved forever in our beauty. So—we would like to work together with you to make it perfect."

The raven straightened. "What did you say?"

"We'd be happy to cooperate, so long as we can give the world a good smile—a bit of butterfly pride—to remember us by."

"Pluck my feathers . . ." the raven said, turning around with a gasp and clasping his hands. "That's the most sensible thing I believe I've ever heard. And all of you feel this way?"

"I'm afraid the other insects may not feel the same way— only the butterflies, your ravenness," the Monarch answered.

He moved closer to the glass as if to speak a secret. "They're not as beautiful as we are, you see."

"Oh, of course. Perhaps they will feel differently, however, once they see how beautiful you can be. Come now," said the raven, dusting off his knees and hurrying to the box. "This is splendid! I'm so happy you've agreed to cooperate. Let's have you go first, shall we?"

The raven reached in and scooped out the Monarch. As he was lifted out of the box, the old butterfly secretly slapped sticky spider thread on the latch, making it so that it wouldn't lock when the raven shut the lid.

"What a true leader you are!" the raven said. "Pay attention, everyone! You should follow the example of your brave leader."

He sat the Monarch down and began taking his measurements.

"I've been meaning to mention," the Monarch began, trying to hide a side-long glance at the collection box, "those rocks hanging around your neck—are they glass?"

"These old things? Oh, heavens, no. They're called *diamonds*," the raven said, putting a hand to his chest.

"They're quite beautiful, aren't they? I ought to cast you with a few. What do you think?"

The Monarch kept the raven talking as the collection box lid opened slowly and small groups of insects climbed out and hurried away. Some made their way quietly up to the ceiling where the chandelier was bolted, and others crawled silently to the ground. Only the butterflies stayed in the box, their faces pressed against the glass, watching as Westly and his little friend Zug Zug climbed to the edge of the chandelier and began spinning one of the most beautiful webs they had ever seen.

In the nest, the Monarch kept the raven distracted.

"And so there I was, water all down the side of my trousers," said the Monarch, chuckling.

The raven was giggling too. "Oh, how embarrassing. How did you ever get out of it?"

"Well, the solution was quite simple, really. Rather than try to towel off in front of all the butterflies, I just took another pitcher of nectar and poured it over the rest of my pants! Soaked clean through! Ha ha! And no one was any the wiser."

"Oh my!" the raven laughed, spilling a little blue resin on the table. "Brilliant. I've got to remember that one. You know, one day everyone will look at me, too. I wonder if I'll handle fame half so well. You'll bring me luck, won't you?"

"Well, certainly," the Monarch bellowed, letting out a merry laugh.

"The resin isn't quite ready. Tell me another story of being a king."

~~~

The web was coming along nicely. Working together, Westly instructed the insects to stretch the threads along the underside of the chandelier, while those on the ceiling worked quickly to chew through the ties that held the fixture secure. In the nest, the raven and the Monarch were working on how the Monarch would pose. He'd chosen to stand with his upper right hand within the fold of his vest, his lower right hand holding back his cloak so it could fall down over his shoulder.

"What do you think?" the raven asked, holding up a small but elaborate hand mirror.

"I believe it suits me well," the Monarch replied, snapping his wings out for full display.

"Excellent! So do I. Can I say I'm so glad we've had this time to chit chat? I'll hold you next to my heart always," the raven said, removing a medal from his chest to show where the king would be.

"What an honor," the Monarch replied, bowing deeply, partly to hide the sweat forming on his brow.

A faint sound of crystals tinkling came from somewhere deep within the chandelier.

The Monarch heaved a sigh of relief, and then he straightened and slapped a palm across his forehead. "Oh! Speaking of medals, I can't believe I didn't remember. The royal headdress—my crown! I couldn't possibly be remembered without my crown. No one would know I was the king!"

"Quite right!" the raven exclaimed. "Would you like to go and fetch it?"

"Absolutely! But I'm still a prisoner. Should I really go alone? I could escape, you know."

"Such a smart butterfly! I appreciate your honesty. Very well, then. Let's go and get it together."

The Monarch smiled. "I left it in the auditorium, near the bottom of the chandelier."

"Of course, of course," the raven said as he took the Monarch's hand. "I'm sorry now about all that unexpected commotion I had to cause. It really was the only way."

"Not to worry, all is forgiven," the Monarch said.

The raven picked him up and swooped out of the nest. All of the insects held their breath as the big bird glided around and around the large chandelier. From his spot in the tree branches, Westly watched as his father guided the raven just below the dangling crystals. Then he heard his father shout, "It's down there, your ravenness."

For a moment, the raven hesitated, and it felt as if time stopped. Had the raven sensed the trap? Would they be turned into jewels anyway?

After a moment of hesitation, the raven tucked in his wings and dove, crashing right into the almost invisible web. The raven yelled and dropped the Monarch, who was able to snap his wings open before he tumbled to the ground.

"Pull!" Westly shouted, as the raven's weight drew the threads tight. Everyone yanked hard. "Chew through now!" Westly shouted at the insects on the ceiling, and with frantic jaws they began to cut the last of the cords holding the chandelier in place.

With a snap and a crash, the large crystal chandelier fell from the ceiling, taking the raven with it as it smashed into the well below, where it lodged in the opening. The bent metal formed what looked like a cage around the top of the rotting wood and stone. Throngs of butterflies, their glass cages smashed, fluttered up out of the well and through the bars of the chandelier. The raven snapped at a few with his beak, but without a net to catch them, his efforts were in vain. The insects all held their breath as the raven, tangled in Westly's web, looked up at them with angry red eyes.

Chapter 20

"Very tricky," the raven growled. He gave the bars of his new prison a shake, but the chandelier did not budge.

When it became clear that the raven couldn't escape, the insects began cheering. "We did it!" the insects shouted as they danced in circles. "We've trapped him!" The butterflies landed and joined the celebration.

While everyone was dancing, Westly watched the raven as he tested the bars of his trap atop the well. He remembered the worms and wondered if the noise had wakened them. With a sinking stomach, Westly realized that the raven was in mortal peril.

Part of Westly wanted to run over and help. He'd never wanted to hurt the raven; he only wanted to free his friends and get the bird out of the menagerie. But his legs remained frozen.

Westly was scared that the raven might tell everyone that

he had let him into the menagerie and caused all this trouble.
But could he just leave the raven to his fate?

Over at the well, the raven was snarling at the insects,
reaching through the bars to grab at them, but they danced
and laughed just out of his reach. Westly could hear the groan
of rotting wood deep in the well, making his heart beat faster.
Whatever secrets he had, Westly had to save the raven from
such an awful fate.

Taking a deep breath, Westly bolted
out of the tangled vines where he'd
been hiding. "You're in danger, Mr.
Raven! Stop moving, or the chandelier will fall!" Westly cried.

To the others he shouted,
"Quick, get him out of there! He'll
die if we don't!" At this sudden
outburst everyone froze, even the
raven.

"Westly?" the Monarch, who
had joined the insects near the
well, said. "What are you doing?"

"Father, you don't understand!

The well is more dangerous than you can imagine! We can't leave him in there!"

"Westly!" the raven whispered. "Westly . . . my little spider!" The insects' mouths dropped open.

"There's no time to explain, Mr. Raven. You're in great danger. I'll help you but you have to promise not to hurt anyone—and leave the menagerie forever!"

"I should have realized it! It was your web that trapped me!" The raven laughed as he pulled at the web that clung to the tatters of his robes. "It's my fault, really. I trained you well."

"Westly—is this true?" the Monarch exclaimed. "You two know each other?"

The raven glanced at Westly and his father. "Know each other?" he repeated. "Why, of course we know each other! I taught him to be a spider."

A cry of disbelief rang through the insects.

"It's true, Father. I, he . . . accepted me like this," Westly said. The smell coming from the well seemed to be getting stronger. "But it doesn't matter now. He's in great danger. We've got to get him out of there!"

"Listen to him, my friends," the raven replied. "I am in danger! I'm worried that this well will collapse and take me down into its dark and dangerous depths forever. You must help me!"

"Do you promise not to hurt anyone?" Westly demanded.

"Of course, Westly. If you'll let me out of this place, I promise to leave you all in peace," he said, placing a wingtip solemnly over his heart.

Westly dashed to the rim of the chandelier, placed six hands on the bent rim, and commanded, "Quick, everyone! Ready—and—heave!" No hands pulled along with him. He turned around.

All the insects stood where they were before, their eyes full of mistrust.

"What have you done, Westly?" the Monarch barked.

"You mean all this was your fault to begin with?" Sara asked.

"It was *you* who let him in here . . . ?" the dragonfly asked. Westly shivered under his glare.

"Why?" the Monarch asked.

"Y-you don't understand," Westly stammered. "H-he was my friend. Or at least I thought he was. But still, we can't leave him like this!" Westly paused. He could hear a hauntingly familiar sound coming from the well. Frightened, he looked down and saw the twisting bodies of the worms waiting just beyond the sunlight. "Please," Westly pleaded. "We must hurry!"

With his back turned, Westly hadn't realized how close he was to the raven until a black wing scooped him up.

"Actually, it doesn't matter if they help," the raven growled as he lifted Westly up to his angry red eyes. "I will get out of this ridiculous cage and then I will turn every one of you into jewels, starting with you, my little *friend*."

The Monarch and Sara ran forward at the same time. "No! Westly! Leave him alone!"

The raven barked out an evil laugh as he used his other wing to pull at the broken chandelier. Bent metal groaned and began to give way. Beneath the insects, the ground rumbled and the rocks of the well started to crumble. Westly looked down and saw the worms getting closer. He could hear them whispering.

The insects heard the worms before the raven did and realized that the creatures in the well were real and not just a child's story. On fluttering wings and hopping legs they grabbed onto the chandelier and began to pull.

Confused, the raven looked at Westly. "What's going on?" he growled.

"We're saving you," Westly said. "We're saving us!"

For a moment the raven hesitated, then his red eyes narrowed. "I don't need you to save me," he spit. "I'll save myself," he said, rattling the bars. "And I will have every one of you."

Just then one whole side of the well crumbled; the wood snapped into dust. The chandelier tipped. The raven looked around surprised. "What . . . what's happening?" he shouted. "What's this?" When he saw the worms sucking at his talons, his beak dropped open and real fear filled his eyes.

"Don't you know? We're the worms," the creatures hissed.

"What's that? Who—?"

"We hear you, little dearie," the worms whispered as one. "You smell like us. You taste like us. And we want you to join us forever."

"Let go of me," the raven shouted, fighting against the worms as they slithered around his legs. "Don't . . . don't touch me!"

"Pull!" Westly commanded. "Everyone, you must pull!"

With all their strength, the insects tried to keep the chandelier from slipping, but the weight was too much for them. The raven slammed against the cage one last time and it began to fall as the well collapsed. With a scream, the raven let go of Westly, who grabbed the edge of a slimy piece of wood with two of his sharp feet and clung tightly. He watched in horror as the cage and the raven and the worms dropped into the darkness.

But before he could sigh with relief, another rumble reminded Westly that he was still in danger. He looked for a way out as the well began crumbling around him, but before he could shout, a happy buzzing circled his head. Zug Zug handed him the edge of a thread, then flew beside him as his friends and family pulled him quickly to safety.

A moment later, the rest of the well collapsed in on itself, sealing up the black hole—and the raven inside it—forever.

ꙮ ～ ꙮ

For a moment, Westly simply lay face down in the dirt. Tears streaked his face and his heart was full. On one hand, he was relieved to see the raven go, but on the other he had a lot to answer for. He had caused all of this destruction.

He lifted himself up slowly and raised his eyes to those around him—his father, Sara, the dragonfly, the centipede, even little Zug Zug.

"I'm sorry," Westly began. "I was so worried about being liked that I forgot about the danger. I knew I shouldn't have talked to the raven, but I did because, well . . . because he was the only one who seemed to care about me. As it turned out he just wanted to get inside the menagerie." Westly broke down. "I'm so sorry." He buried his face in his hands and cried.

A warm, friendly arm pulled him close. "It's all right, Wes," his father said.

"Do not doubt for a second the difference you made," he heard the dragonfly say.

"You saved us," Sara said.

The Monarch tilted Westly's chin up until the sad little spider was looking at him. "We have no control over the color of our wings—or how many legs we have. Nor does life always turn out the way we planned," the Monarch said. "We can only do the best with what we've been given. You were meant to be different, Westly. Not only did your differences save us, but they brought two groups back together as one family!" he said, looking at the dragonfly.

Westly wiped a tear from his eye and replied softly, "But I messed up. The menagerie will never be the same. It's all my fault."

Westly's father knelt so he could look into his son's eyes. "Messing up is part of growing up."

Crying softly, his voice barely a whisper, Westly replied, "I just wanted to be a butterfly, Dad. I just wanted to make you proud."

"Oh, my beautiful Westly. Oh, my beautiful boy," the Monarch said, a tear of his own falling down his cheek, "you are more than a butterfly. And there is no father that could be more proud of his son than I am."

Without another word, Westly stepped forward and wrapped all his arms around his father.

All around, the insects cheered. A happy little fly buzzed

around them all. At the edge of the crowd, a blind moth
smiled.

Epilogue

The blind moth sat on the edge of an ivy leaf. Dipped low to the ground, he was surrounded by a new batch of caterpillars, ant larvae, and other young insects. His fuzzy hair had long since turned white with age, and his antennae drooped just a bit. Though his legs were steady, he propped himself up with a hand-carved staff.

Below him, the children listened to his words with wonder.

"Things were forever changed from that day on," he said, finishing his story about the little caterpillar that had turned into a spider. "The butterflies had lost their home and their flowers. And we gardeners, our fields were shredded, the menagerie door was broken, our food dashed to pieces—we even had the fearful task of teaching butterflies how to take care of themselves.

"But despite the problems Westly had caused, there was never a single complaint against him. You see, he was right, standing out on the beach in the cold that day. We couldn't have become who we were meant to be had we left the butterflies—our family. Together, our menagerie did indeed grow more in peace and friendship than it ever could have otherwise. And just as the butterflies had originally intended, when the time came, they crowned Westly as their Monarch."

"I love that story," one of the larvae whispered to a caterpillar.

"Me too," another agreed.

The moth smiled. "Do any of you remember what Westly's first royal action was?" One of the baby grasshoppers raised his hand.

"Yes, Alvin?"

"He let the caterpillars eat and eat and eat until the sunlight came back."

"That's correct. It took a long time, but gradually the sunlight shone into even the most lost and forbidden corners. The carnivorous plants withered away, the fog dried up, and the streams ran clear. We built a new garden over the hole where the well once stood, and this new home became a place where both butterflies and gardeners could live together in peace. Its roots grew deep and true, washing away all the blackness. And now, years later, delicious flowers grow from the top of the atrium all the way to the tip of the menagerie door."

The old moth stepped down off the leaf and made his way

carefully through the group of children, pausing to add just one more thing. "Never forget, children, we have all of this because a little black spider learned that being different isn't such a bad thing, and even misfits can grow up to be heroes."

And with that, the old moth wandered off into the tall green grass.

Acknowledgments

Amanda, thank you for that one brush stroke you made on page 99 while we were chatting about nothing on a Saturday night. I'm so glad we can now say that you're my co-illustrator. Also, thank you for being more than anything any man could ever ask for in a wife.

My mother's mother, for holding back my emotional matches all those times I was so frustrated I wanted to burn this project to the ground.

My father's mother, for being a stellar example of hard work and love.

Westley Beus, my young nephew, for so willingly sharing with Westly your name—and even before asking, "Am I a good guy or a bad guy?"

Chris, Joe, Hannah, Kim, and Katie, thank you for being supportive siblings as I've worked.

Kristie Bennion and Justin Pederson, for being my second family.

Chris Schoebinger, for taking this huge risk on me, and for keeping the vision clear through the many years of development.

Heidi Taylor. Oh, Heidi, the number of things you've done to make this project successful is innumerable. Thank you. You win every award for "Best Editor Ever Ever Ever."

Richard Erickson, for being such a pleasant and easy-going art director.

Ryan Woodward, for giving up one lunch break after another to help a struggling student. Thank you for believing in me.

Brad Holland, for teaching me that when all is finished, '. . . It's still just a painting . . .'

Steve Richins, for those seven years of weekly private saxophone lessons, in which the real thing you taught was not how to make beautiful music, but how to be a listener.

Richard Ferre, for helping me as I try to understand that who I am is exactly who I am supposed to be.

Erik and Emily Orton, for being there.

Don Seegmiller, for helping me learn from my mistakes.

Bjorn Pendleton, for giving me my first start as an illustrator.

Gregory Manchess and Irene Gallo, perhaps you remember the time I absentmindedly usurped an entire Friday evening which you two had planned to spend together. Thank you for being so kind in the way you treated me that it wasn't until years later that I realized how rude my behavior was. It left a lasting impression on me on the nature and meaning of being a storyteller.

Others:

Holly Dustin Richins, Lisa Mangum, Jenni James, Steven Hendricks, Ray Smith, Robert Barrett, Bethanne Anderson, Richard Hull, Kelly Loosli, LTUE, Salt Lake Comic Con, Blake Casselman, David and Jane Fjeldsted, Benjamin Nordby, Andrew Allen, Jordan Fowers, all my extended family, all my roommates over the years, Bruce Allred and Tom Householder, Nathan Crenshaw, Berin Stephens, Stephen Gashler, Brady Dalton, Jaren Peterson, Nathan Gomm, Ryan Butcher, Sal Scaramado, Kayla Hackett, and Richard Solomon.

And thank you, dear reader, for taking the chance to read Westly's story. It's one that I feel is worth the long effort it took to record it on paper. I hope that you think so, too.